ID:

THE MAN
WITH
TWO LIVES

Vincent J. Sachar

SPECIAL THANKS

To everyone who has the courage and creativity to release their imagination—the most powerful force that we all possess. This is what transforms a black and white world to color.

To my wife, Gwen, for her invaluable support, encouragement, and collaboration.

"Imagination is the beginning of creation. You imagine what you desire, you will what you imagine, and at last you create what you will." — George Bernard Shaw

Table of Contents

Chapter One: The Impossible Happens...........................1

Chapter Two: Between Two Lives 8

Chapter Three: The Need to Know........................14

Chapter Four: A Storm is Brewing 21

Chapter Five: Taking Another Step.......................28

Chapter Six: It's Getting Hotter........................37

Chapter Seven: Gotta Get Proactive......................44

Chapter Eight: Back at the Office 50

Chapter Nine: Beyond My Limits 56

Chapter Ten: Already in Prison......................62

Chapter Eleven: Imagine This.......................69

Chapter Twelve: Minutes Turn into Seconds 77

Chapter Thirteen: Ugh! Rehabilitation 83

Chapter Fourteen: And So It Goes.....................90

From the Author: 94

About the Author: 95

Chapter One

The Impossible Happens

H ow do you explain the inexplicable? When all that is ordinary and established in your life suddenly flees without warning, you're left in the wake as unable to explain things as anyone else. Losing a job or possessions can be catastrophic. Losing your identity and suddenly finding that everyone else sees you as someone you are not is beyond definition.

That pretty much describes my feelings on that day when I became a completely different person. I know that sounds strange and you may already be judging my lucidity. Believe me, you will not be the first person to question whether something has slipped out of gear in my mind. I have questioned that myself. But, hear me out. I am telling you this as honestly as I possibly can. Overnight, I have become, at least to everyone but myself, a completely different person.

When I look in the mirror, I see me or, I should say, the me I used to be. I see Jeff Norman. I am thirty-eight years old, five feet eleven inches tall. I have brown hair, green eyes, and a lean body. But, I apparently am the only person on Earth who sees that person. Everyone else sees me as Avery Douglas, a thirty-six-year-old, wavy-haired blonde with hazel eyes, who

1

stands at six feet two inches with a solid body. The driver's license and its photo in my wallet say I am Avery Douglas. The gorgeous five feet six-inch tall, thirty-four-year-old brunette with captivating blue eyes, inviting lips, and a curvaceous body identifies me as her husband. Her name is Kathleen Douglas and, let me tell you, it is difficult to believe she has given birth to two children. Oh yeah, kids. Did I mention that Kathleen and I purportedly have two children?

Melissa is twelve and Jalen is eight-years-old. I am their loving father, despite the fact that I never laid eyes on them until after I first saw them following several days of unconsciousness in the hospital. Even so, they both seem to know me.

As Jeff Norman, I was single, no children, and lived in a comfortable two-bedroom condominium. I was approaching my fifteenth year as a UPS driver.

As Avery Douglas, in addition to having a wife and two children, I live in an elegant five-bedroom home with an indoor pool in a gated community. Apparently, I am a successful investment broker of some sort.

As I told you from the outset, this is all so preposterous that I have, for the moment, stopped denying that I am not Avery Douglas until I find some way to understand it all. I don't want to end up in some psycho ward, donning a straight-jacket, never wearing a belt, and forced to use plastic forks, spoons, and knives.

My last memory as Jeff Norman was losing control of my car on an icy road. I remember heading uncontrollably towards a stone wall. My first moment as Avery Douglas was when I opened my eyes while lying in a hospital bed with Kathleen fawning over me.

A burly nurse, with no apparent neck, was telling me to remain still while she summoned a doctor.

Even more perplexing, the road I was driving on was situated in Maple Grove, Minnesota. With a population of slightly more than 60,000, Maple Grove's claim to fame is that it boasts one of the Twin Cities largest shopping centers, The Shoppes at Arbor Lakes. The hospital where I woke is in Miramar, Florida, some 1,800 miles away. I had never even been in this city before in my life.

My primary injuries, beyond bruises and contusions, consisted of trauma to the head and a severe concussion. Ironically, this and the fact that I was in at least a semicomatose state for several days, aided me greatly when I initially expressed such deep confusion concerning my identity.

"Just give your husband some time," Doctor Prabodh Badal told Kathleen. "He has experienced a great deal of trauma to his head. There is still so very much about head injuries that we do not understand. You're just going to have to be patient. I am going to recommend psychiatric therapy designed to assist your husband, as well as assisting you, in knowing how to deal with this."

I was released from the hospital after an extended stay and a slew of tests. I have already had a session with Dr. Marion Westinghouse. She is a medical psychiatrist who has spent most of her time trying to convince me that I am not crazy and will soon be settled in with who I am. Little does she know. I want to tell her that she's the one who's crazy for thinking that my brain is going to chill and accept my Avery Douglas identity. Fortunately, I have, at least, been sane enough not to call a medical psychiatrist crazy.

3

Nevertheless, the problem remains. If I tell Dr. Westinghouse that I do know my true identity and it is not Avery Douglas, we could be talking about me taking residency in some looney bin learning how to make candles or crochet woolen scarves and mittens. And scarves and mittens will be of no use or value in south Florida.

One advantage of my head injuries is the fact that I will not be returning to work until I am released by my doctor to do so. Since I know absolutely nothing about investment brokering, I have been spared from discovery as a blatant fraud.

Even before I left the hospital, I realized that no one was going to spend any time whatsoever trying to unravel the incredible mystery of how I somehow entered into another person's identity. That task was mine and mine alone.

Upon my return home, I was determined to do my own investigation. My initial approach was to enter into my, or should I say, Avery's study and begin searching online. My first challenge was that I did not know the password that would provide access to Avery's account. There was one saving grace, however. I noticed that the computer had designated locations for Avery's personal account, Kathleen's account, and a guest account. The accounts for Avery and Kathleen were password protected. The guest account was not. I would have preferred to access Avery's personal account and learn more about him or... uh... myself, but that would simply have to come at another time. For now, I needed Internet access and the opportunity to explore.

In listening to the doctors, I learned that Avery Douglas had also been in an auto accident at the same time as me. I began by searching for recent accidents that occurred here in south Florida. I found the accident that Douglas had been in quite readily only because it involved three other vehicles in which the driver of one car and a passenger were killed. Three of the four passengers in the other two vehicles were reported to be in serious, but not life-threatening condition. Avery Douglas, who had been traveling alone in his current year Maserati Gran Turismo Sport, was one of the victims listed in serious, but stable condition. Nothing more was said about the condition of the super-expensive Maserati.

I then began investigating a same day accident that would have occurred in the vicinity of the Twin Cities in Minnesota. I initially found nothing, but, as I continued to dig, I finally came across a one-car accident involving Jeff Norman. The report said that Norman was victimized by "black ice" at night while driving in Brooklyn Park, Minnesota. That's a community located about eight miles northeast of Maple Grove. Norman was driving his four-year-old Ford Fusion when he lost control of his car and slammed into a rock wall that surrounded the personal property of a homeowner in that area. The last report stated that Jeff Norman had severe cranial swelling and had been placed in a medically-induced coma.

My body shook as I uncovered this information. Based upon what I had learned, the real me was purportedly laid up in a coma in Maple Grove Hospital, while the "Avery Douglas me" was back home with my beautiful wife and two children. My mind began to race with a myriad of confusing, even frightening, thoughts.

Was all of this simply a dream nestled in the mind of someone asleep in a medically-induced coma? So, maybe there is no Avery Douglas and he and this existence only exist in my warped comatose mind. Or maybe I am dead and temporarily caught somewhere between two worlds? Or maybe I am like the man-in-black in the movie, "Princess Bride," and am only "mostly dead."

Within minutes, my body was soaked in perspiration and my head ached. I had honestly resolved nothing, but I knew that I had to stop for now. Man, talk about head trauma, whatever I was now experiencing had to be worse than a concussion.

Just then, Kathleen entered the room.

"Oh Avery, darling, you are soaked with perspiration. You must have overextended yourself. You need to stop. Get some rest, honey. Both Dr. Badal and Dr. Westinghouse have stated that you will need to initially pace yourself. You simply can't do too much too soon."

Then, she leaned forward and kissed my neck. The kiss surprised me, but I managed not to recoil from the confusion in my mind that Kathleen was married to Avery Douglas and not to me.

I responded to Kathleen by getting up from my chair and walking into the living room. I sat down on the couch, elevated my legs, and welcomed the cold glass of ice tea that Kathleen gave to me.

I reasoned that I could still be in a comatose state and what I was experiencing now was nothing more than the manufactured dreams of a fractured mind. I honestly could not fathom that through some force or forces unknown to me, I had somehow switched bodies with another man and was presently captive to an identity that was not my own?

You might say that living in a million-dollar home, with a gorgeous wife, two sweet children, and enough money to afford a freakin' Maserati, is not a bad deal at all. I mean, if I were to suddenly find myself in someone else's identity, I most certainly could have fared a lot worse than this. But the problem was that I was now living a lie and I alone knew it.

As I reflected further, I realized that I had no explanation as to how any of this had occurred. I shuddered when I acknowledged that I also had no way of knowing if or when it would ever end.

Chapter Two

Between Two Lives

As I passed the three-week mark of my new existence, I lived with the notion that I would wake up someday soon and find that all I was experiencing now was nothing more than a trick being played against my own mind. Hah! I was trying to convince myself that this Avery guy and his wife and family likely did not even exist. At least I knew that a place named Miramar in south Florida was not fictitious. But, maybe I had read about it somewhere at some time in my life. We all know that the mind can be a very complex thing. For a few days, I lived with the expectation that this was all going to end very soon and I would be back delivering packages for Brown in Minnesota.

Unfortunately, I simply could not hold onto that belief for very long. If this was nothing more than a figment of my imagination, I was more than ready for it to end. If, as incredible as it seemed, this was real, I had to know how and why this occurred. I could not continue to live in such a state of bewilderedness. Besides, I had some pretty elaborate dreams in my lifetime, but nothing was ever so clear and logically sequential as this. Whatever this was, I was living every minute and hour of every day and not bouncing around as dreams normally do.

I quickly learned that Kathleen was a beautiful person in more ways than her physical appearance. She was kind, gentle, intelligent, and loving. I avoided any significant intimacy with her, despite my desires, since I knew in my heart she was a wife, but not mine. Dr. Westinghouse informed me that she had advised Kathleen not to rush intimacy with me, but rather to reestablish a close bond and trust.

I also caught on to the fact that Melissa and Jalen were much more strongly attached to their mom than to dad. I wondered if Avery might be a workaholic who simply did not spend a great deal of time with his own children. Guess if you're going to make mega-bucks, some things in your life are going to suffer.

It was on a Saturday morning that I received the first major surprise in my life as Avery Douglas. Kathleen and the children were out shopping and I was sitting in the study when the call came into my cell phone. I answered with a simple, "Hello."

"Avery, oh my God, it's you. Can you talk, darling? Is anyone with you?"

Great, a voice on the phone and nothing in my contacts to help me identify the caller.

"Uh, yes, I... uh... I can talk. No, no one else is here. Kathleen and the kids are out shopping."

"Oh, Avery. Oh, my darling. I have been worried sick over you. I didn't dare show up at the hospital for fear that she might be there. I was so scared, my love. I thought that I might lose you. Are you all right, baby? Are you okay?"

Nothing in my false identity gave me a clue as to who this person was, except that it did not take much to realize that Mr. Avery Douglas had another woman in his life. I mean this woman did not speak as a sister or close relative would, nor in the manner of a co-worker. Whoever this person was, she was obviously in a role that would not play favorably with Avery's wife.

Great, here I am fighting the urge to get intimate with Kathleen and I have some unknown lover who is also in my life.

It is so very difficult to find a way to get a person whom you supposedly know, a person with whom you have been intimate, a person who sees herself as your lover, to somehow reveal her name. I mean what am I supposed to say? "You don't know how incredibly much I have missed you, how much I have longed to hold you in my arms and kiss you—by the way, what is your name again?"

We ended the call with me talking about my serious head injury, ongoing doctor care, and the fact that I would continue to be laid up for a while.

She ended the conversation by assuring me she would more than make up for the time gap when we are together again. I responded to her sworn oaths of love for me by saying things like "Me too" and other phrases that purportedly returned my feelings for her. Incredible! I had absolutely no idea who I was talking to or even what she looked like, but I was forced to receive and reciprocate to pledges birthed out of love or lust.

In my life as Jeff Norman, I had never married, sired any children, or been intimately involved with the wife of another man. My latest girlfriend, Alicia, and I dated for nearly eight years and actually lived together for about five of those years. It was my unwillingness to take the next step and marry her that led to our breakup.

I cannot explain just what it was in me that caused me to hold back from marrying Alicia. I cannot even cite a list of things about her that troubled, bothered, or disappointed me.

"I will always have a love for you," she told me on that last day, "but I want to find a man who understands true commitment and is willing to take those next steps."

Last I heard, Alicia did find that someone and was engaged to be married.

Now I suddenly find myself supposedly married with children and, at least, one lover on the side.

André, that is correct, freakin' André from *Premier Luxury Vehicles,* called later that same day to confirm that they had received full authorization from an insurer to repair my Maserati. In the interim, since they did not have a Maserati at the level of my Gran Turismo Sport, they were offering me a year-old Lamborghini Aventador as a replacement while my car was being repaired.

André, I repeat the car dude was, in fact, named André, said that Phillipé and Willie, go figure, would come by my home to drop off my temporary wheels. Okay, so André did not actually refer to the vehicle as "wheels," but the whole thing was so preposterous to me that, even now, I strive for some semblance of normalcy.

Kathleen and the children were back home when the replacement vehicle arrived. When I informed Kathleen that I wanted to take the car for a ride, she was very concerned. Who knows? Perhaps she was afraid I would get lost or maybe forget which pedal was the brake and which was the accelerator.

In any event, I assured her I would be fine. The car and my cell phone both had a GPS and, if I had any problem, whatsoever, I would simply call home. And yes, I had already checked and my cell had a listed number for home and for Kathleen's cell.

There's no question that I had never driven a Lamborghini before or a car anywhere close to that level, but, at the moment, I was not focused upon that at all. Being alone driving a car provided me with an opportunity to reflect upon all that had transpired in my life. Nothing made sense at all. I even considered that I really was Avery Douglas and Jeff Norman was some fictitious character of my mind.

In any event, I was riding along just kind of cruising through local neighborhoods when I suddenly realized that a black Suburban with dark-tinted windows seemed to be following me. At first, I assumed that it was simply my imagination. After all, maybe I did not understand a whole lot of what was going on in my life, but I did at least know that some things had been knocked loose in my head. It stands to reason, I would be imagining all sorts of things.

Imaginations and loose items in my head notwithstanding, I pulled into a quick stop and was relieved when the suspicious Suburban drove by and disappeared from view. I smiled, sighed, and turned around to head back home. As I did, I had to admit that the Lamborghini Aventador is honestly one really awesome set of wheels... uh... I mean luxury vehicle. Perhaps, I could get used to driving luxury vehicles. I had to admit they provided a much smoother ride than the truck I drove for a living.

Cruising around in a Lamborghini generated both a positive and negative result for me. On the plus side, I found myself relaxing in ways that I had been unable to do ever since I found myself mysteriously locked into someone else's life. For the first time in weeks, I let go of my inner struggles and simply enjoyed the fact that I was alive.

On the negative side, it was not until much later that I realized that the strange black Suburban had resumed its mission of following me.

Chapter Three

The Need to Know

I was continually pounding my brain, no longer focused upon how this all occurred, but, rather, upon what, if anything, could I do about it. For the life of me, I could not think of anyone I could turn to, anyone who might believe my story—at least not anyone credible. I mean, I knew there were supermarket tabloids that would jump on a story like this or perhaps some conspiracy buffs who would somehow try to prove that I had an encounter with aliens. All of this left me feeling incredibly isolated, alone, and, utterly helpless.

I had an idea, but I wasn't sure just how I would be able to carry it out. I had the sense that before the accident, Avery Douglas did what he wanted, when he wanted, with little or no "say-so" from Kathleen. That was simply my impression, but I felt reasonably sure that's how things were. Now, Kathleen, evidencing her kind heart, had taken on a much more protective role on behalf of her confused husband.

I sat with her one evening and told her that I was beginning to feel more clarity in my mind. I lied telling her that past events and occurrences were beginning to surface in my thoughts and that I even had a glimpse or two of the accident that I was involved in.

"I have an idea, Kathleen. I think that if I can sit alone in a quiet setting, it might help me to further clear my mind. In fact, I'm thinking I'll pack a light snack or two, bring some bottled water, and settle in somewhere for the day tomorrow."

I was elated when Kathleen bought into the idea, as long as I promised to check in with her a few times to assure that all was well.

I had already looked into the flight schedules to Minnesota and was sure that I could fly out and back without Kathleen knowing I had ever left the area. I felt a little guilty that I would be using Avery's Platinum American Express Card to pay for things, but I had no alternative... uh... other than using one of his other five or so credit cards. Look, I didn't ask to somehow end up inside the guy's identity. At the moment, like I said, I really had no other choice.

As I said, I had already checked for flights. My options were lousy. In order to accomplish what I intended to do, my best bet was to fly out of Miami at 5:45 a.m. That would get me to Chicago O'Hare at 8:10 a.m. With a fifty-five- minute layover, we'd be back in the air at 9:05 a.m. and on the ground at the St. Paul International Airport in Minneapolis at 10:40 a.m. I would then pick up a rental car at the airport to get me to Maple Grove and back for my return flight.

Kathleen was a sound sleeper. Besides, I had been sleeping in the guest bedroom under the pretense that my sleep was still restless and I was prone to wake up during the night and turn a light on and read. Of course, when I first mentioned this to Kathleen, she giggled saying she had never seen me read a book

15

throughout the entirety of our marriage. In any event, Kathleen would go along with just about anything if she thought it might help me get well again.

Needless to say, sleeping in the guest room helped immensely when I rose up and left the house at around 4:00 a.m. and made the trek to the airport. As expected, traffic was light at such an ungodly hour of the morning. Even so, I wondered why anyone, other than me, would even be on the roads at a time like this.

When I purchased my tickets and used the credit card, and, again, when I passed through security, I kind of half-expected that bells and buzzers would go off and I would be revealed as a fraud using someone else's identity. None of that ever happened. Once again, to everyone in the world, except me, I was Avery Douglas.

My first flight was right on schedule. I hardly had time for a cup of coffee in Chicago before I was in the air again and headed for Minneapolis. It was a Saturday morning, so Melissa and Jalen would not be getting up for school and Kathleen would stay in bed until at least 10:00 or 10:30. So, I was feeling pretty good. Of course, 10:00 a.m. or 10:30 a.m. would be 9:00 a.m. or 9:30 a.m. Chicago time and I would be either boarded on my next flight or in the air. So, I texted Kathleen around 9:30 a.m., her time, told her I was awake and headed out and would contact her again once I settled in on where I was going to be. I figured that would buy me some time before my next deceitful text had to be sent.

I was calm and relaxed until I was parking my rental car at the Maple Grove Hospital. I didn't know what to think or what to feel. The real me was purportedly lying in a coma within the walls of this hospital and I was on my way hoping that I could somehow steal a glimpse of Jeff Norman... or... uh... me. There was a part of me that was afraid and wanted to simply start the car up and drive away. There was another part of me that questioned why in the world I was even doing this. Yet, there was also a part of me that just had to know.

I had done some research before heading to Minnesota. I read where many comatose patients stay in a hospital's intensive care unit so that doctors and nurses can continually monitor them. I knew that would make it extremely difficult, if not impossible, for me to get access to even see Jeff Norman. But, I had to try. I had to find a way. Like I said, I just had to know.

As I approached the hospital's ICU, I spotted the sign. "Only immediate family members admitted to visit ICU patients." I was outside the hospital's ICU trying desperately to conjure up a way to get into the area where Jeff Norman was located when all the pressure, confusion, and turmoil just seemed to come to a head. I sat down in a chair and I began to sob. Tears were pouring from my eyes. I felt so lost, so confused, so empty.

In the midst of all that, I never heard her approach. She sat down next to me, placed a hand on my shoulder, and spoke to me. Her words sounded as if they were coming from another room. They bore a slight echo. They were gentle and immediately reached inside of me.

When I lifted my head, the first thing I spotted through my blurred vision was her nametag, "Doris M. Sharpely, R.N." I lifted my head further and caught sight of this elderly woman, her glasses hanging on a chain around her neck, her eyes gray, yet warm and inviting.

"What is it, sir? How may I help you? I am Nurse Sharpely. I work here at the hospital. Is there something I can do for you? Some way I can assist you?"

My initial thought was simply an awareness that I was in the presence of a very kindhearted, maternal woman who likely epitomized the profession of care and concern to which she had dedicated her life.

I paused for a moment, then spoke.

"I-I came here hoping that somehow I could have just a moment to see my... my dear friend, Jeff. He's here in ICU in a coma."

"Oh, I am so sorry, sir, but hospital rules do limit visitation to immediate family members. You mentioned your friend, Jeff? Are you referring to Mr. Norman? Mr. Jeff Norman?"

I looked up again into her eyes and nodded my head. Then, suddenly, I began to lie. As I did, I realized that everything in and about my life was nothing more than a lie. Throughout each day, everything about me, everything I said or did was birthed in deceitfulness. That's all I was. I was a fraud—a man who, under the circumstances, could pretty much never tell the truth. In a relatively short amount of time, I was becoming increasingly skilled, very adept at lying.

"Jeff's my very best friend. I-I've known him my entire life. I... uh... well, I've been working overseas, in Europe, on assignment for my company. I just got back in the States and will be headed back to London again. I-I just wanted to see him before I leave the country, in case... in case... I might n-never get to ever see him again. I just wanted to stand at his bed and just look upon his face for just a moment. I... "

"Shh... hold still. Just a moment and wait here for me," Nurse Sharpely said.

Within a minute or two she was back with a sign-up sheet attached to a clipboard.

"Quick, let me see your ID."

I pulled my wallet from my pocket, handed her my Florida Drivers License and watched as she wrote everything down on the sheet.

"Just for a minute or two and you must not approach him at all. No touching. Can you do that?"

"Yes," I answered, as I thanked her profusely.

As we entered the ICU, my body was trembling. I honestly did not know what to expect. Would that really be me, my body, lying unconscious, attached to instruments monitoring my vitals and heartbeat, my life appearing as numbers and blips on a monitor near the bed? Or maybe this entire charade would end here when I discover that there is a Jeffrey Norman, but he looks nothing like the man I imagined myself to be. This dude might be ninety years old, or African-American, or nowhere close to the man I have been claiming to be for almost a month.

As we moved closer to the man lying prone here in this hospital, I felt a twinge of relief. Maybe now, all this craziness in my head that I'm actually another person would come to a crashing halt and I would begin to focus and concentrate on finding a way of accepting that I am Avery Douglas and always have been.

Ah, the human mind is such a fragile and deeply complex thing. We cannot actually see it, touch it, nor completely understand or control it. Yet, it steers, guides, and controls our lives. It sometimes causes us to imagine things that simply have no basis in fact.

So, perhaps coming here wasn't such a bad idea after all, especially if this is what it would take to bring me back to my senses and help me to move on with my life.

I cannot even remember the words that Nurse Sharpely spoke as we stood quietly at the bedside of Jeff Norman. Even now everything is a blur. All I remember is that I became lightheaded and tears poured from my eyes.

I knew. As I stood in that room transfixed on a man lying unconscious in a coma, I knew. He was me. He was the person I had always been up until a month or so ago.

Doris Sharpely attributed my reactions to that of a loving friend fearful that he was looking at someone he might never again see alive. The dear woman could not possibly know nor understand that I was in a strange body staring at myself.

Chapter Four

A Storm is Brewing

To be quite honest, I hardly remember the trip back to Florida. I'm actually amazed to think that I somehow drove away from the hospital, back to the airport, surrendered a rented car, boarded a flight, ended up back in Miami, and drove to my home in Miramar.

Somewhere along the line, I remembered to turn my phone back on and spotted the six phone calls and eight texts from Kathleen that had gone unanswered. I sent a quick text apologizing, claiming some problems with my phone, and stating that I was on my way home.

When I entered the house looking like a used dish towel, Kathleen accepted my claim that I had a good day, but had likely pushed myself too far. I informed her that all I wanted now was a shower and an early retirement to bed. Kathleen did not challenge me at all. She never did. I was beginning to sense that her refusal to ever challenge her husband was not simply something that began once he suffered a severe head injury in a car accident. It was the pattern of life that their marriage had evolved into over the years. Avery Douglas was the dominant bully whose lack of affection towards his wife was excused in light of the fact that the man was an excellent provider and a father to their two children. Kathleen Douglas was the perfect example of a wife whose spousal abuse primarily consisted of verbal insults and neglect, rather than any actual corporal punishment. The same was likely true of Avery Douglas' relationship with his two children.

Great, so I was now not only a false husband and father, but a lousy one to boot. I began to seriously wonder just what else I would be learning about the new me. I would soon begin to discover that I had no earthly idea just what I was up against.

~ひ ~ひ ~ひ

Over the next few days, I was relatively quiet at home. Kathleen went about her daily routine of getting the kids off to school, taking Melissa to her dance classes, and making sure Jalen was at his baseball games and practices.

I continued to get a few phone calls from my mysterious lover, who became increasingly explicit in how much she desired to be with me again as soon as possible. But it was actually the call I received one Thursday afternoon that began to dramatically change things. I was sitting alone in a lounge chair next to our indoor pool. Kathleen and the kids were out somewhere doing something when the call came in on my cell phone. The caller was listed as "Unknown."

"Nice to hear your voice, Douglas," the caller said. The voice was deep, masculine, and bore a hint of a northeastern accent. "You know, we been patient while you mend up, my friend, but you best not think you can hide behind some kind of bump on your head forever. You know?"

"Who is this?" I said, before realizing how foolish my question was. The caller acted as if I knew exactly who he was. Apparently, I was supposed to know this man. In fact, it was likely extremely important that I did know.

"I'm warnin' you, Douglas. Don't play any games with me. It ain't a healthy thing to do and I ain't in no frivolous mood, especially when there's a matter of some 300K you need to be sending back our way. The boss, he's been kind enough to respect the fact that you got yourself banged up and all. But I'm sure I don't have to tell you, he ain't somebody you should take for granted."

I felt a cold chill race through my mind and body.

"The clock is runnin', Avery. We been showin' you our good nature by givin' you some time to heal and all, but I'm warnin' you. Don't play with this. Remember, even if I wanted to help you, I don't have total control in everything here. I answer to the boss, just like you.

So, if you wanna be sure that you, your hot wife, and them beautiful kids don't come to no harm, you better start makin' arrangements to get us our money real soon. You hear?"

"Listen, I... "

There was no sense in my continuing to talk. I could see that the caller hung up.

Just that quickly, beads of sweat appeared on my lips and forehead. I was gripping my cell phone so tightly that my knuckles had turned white and my hand began to cramp. I held my breath, then took occasional gulps of air in an effort to somehow regain control of my breathing. My body was shaking so hard that it took a few minutes before I could even stand up.

I had no idea what I should do next. Call the police? Tell them I just received a call from some unknown person who clearly threatened my family, which isn't really my family, and me, despite the fact that I'm not really me, about some money, that I know absolutely nothing about, because I'm really not Avery Douglas at all. No, I'm actually the guy lying in a coma at a hospital in Maple Grove, Minnesota. Yeah, that might work really well.

But, at the same time, the caller clearly made threats against Kathleen, Melissa, and Jalen. An innocent wife and two young children were at risk over something I was quite sure they knew absolutely nothing about. I couldn't simply ignore that and call myself a decent human being.

The caller mentioned money, some three hundred thousand dollars. It could be a gambling debt or even something related to drugs, but I had a feeling that this related to Avery's work as an investment broker. All I knew, only because I heard it mentioned in one of the conversations we were having with the shrink, Dr. Marion Westinghouse, was that Avery Douglas was some kind of investment broker. That had to be the source of the money this caller was referring to. Who knows? Had Avery Douglas embezzled funds or wrongly appropriated money that belonged to others? And who was the guy that called me? Even more importantly, who was the "boss?"

I had to find a way to go to the office where Avery Douglas worked. I had been avoiding this entirely because I feared that would be the time and place where I would most likely be exposed as a complete fraud. If I could even find my office, how would I explain the fact that I knew absolutely no one who worked there with me? And what about the fact that I did not know the first thing about whatever it really was that Avery Douglas did for a living? Worse yet, what if the mysterious caller was someone in the very office that I would be going to? I had to find a way to do this. At the moment, I honestly was completely devoid of any plausible ways to accomplish this.

It was at this point that my strongest inclination was to run, to get away from everyone and everything. If it were not for Kathleen and two innocent children, I would have been gone in a "New York Minute."

Once again, it was an unexpected phone call that changed everything and provided me with the opportunity that I so desperately needed.

~Ω~ ~Ω~ ~Ω~

"Avery, how you doing, buddy?"

This time the caller ID on my phone listed the name of the caller, "Stan Fredrickson"—well, at least, I had a name.

"I waited a while before calling you. Wanted to give you some time to get better. How are you feeling, man? Everything okay?"

"Hi, Stan. Yeah, well, I'm getting there for sure. It's been a bit of a slower road than I anticipated."

"Well, hey, that was a nasty head injury you got there, my friend. You're lucky to be alive, you know?"

"Yeah. Guess I am."

"I visited you at the hospital, but there's no way in hell you'd ever remember that. Man, it scared me when I saw you lying there all hooked up and all.

Anyway, you're not missing much at the office. Same old, same old, you know? By the way, Sid, Marty, and Lois asked me to send along their greetings and best wishes to you."

It struck me like a lightning bolt. Stan Fredrickson was a co-worker. He worked in the same office as me. This could be my answer, my ticket in, my way to visit the office under circumstances that just might permit me to not totally expose my false identity. I decided to go for it.

"Hey, Stan, I wonder if I could ask you to do me a favor?"

"Sure, Avery, just name it. Always glad to help. You know that."

"I want to come into the office. The doctors want me to take things slow. Reacquaint myself with things in my life, you know? I can't return to work yet, until they release me to do so. But I'm thinking it might help me a bit if I could just come in for a short visit. See things again."

"Sure, sure, Avery, how can I help?"

"Well, I was thinking if you would be willing to come pick me up, bring me in."

"Oh my gosh, you kidding, man? Glad to. Just name the day and time."

"But... uh... just one thing, Stan. I... uh... sometimes still get confused. Forget people's names. Things like that. My doctors say those things will clear up eventually and to an extent they already are beginning to," I lied. "But, I wouldn't want to insult anyone."

"Hah, you not insulting people would probably be a first for most people," Stan said, followed by a big laugh. "Nah. No problem at all, Avery. I'll bring you in and stay with you. No problem at all."

"Hey, thanks, Stan. Means a lot. I'll owe you one."

Stan laughed.

"You probably owe me a ton already," he said, while continuing to laugh.

We ended the call with an agreement that Stan would pick me up at my home the next day at 9:30 a.m., bring me into the office, and drive me back whenever I was ready. Once I got to the office, I had no idea what to look for and what, if anything, I might find. All I knew was that I had to keep digging into the life of Avery Douglas as deeply and quickly as possible. As the man said on the phone, the clock was already running.

Chapter Five

Taking Another Step

I had already informed Kathleen that Stan would be bringing me into the office in the morning. I was standing in the kitchen with Kathleen, Melissa, and Jalen when Kathleen mentioned that she and the children were hungry and she had not had time to prepare dinner.

"Well, let's go out somewhere to eat," I said.

My failure to mention a place in particular was based upon the fact that I was unfamiliar with any of the local restaurants. My suggestion was met with silence.

"Well, what's the problem here? Don't any of you want to go out to eat?"

Again, no one said a word.

"What's going on here?" I asked. "Someone come up with a suggestion and let's go. Why do I keep running into a brick wall?"

Melissa was the first one to speak.

"Because you don't like any of the places we ever want to go to," she said.

"Yeah," Jalen answered, "and whenever we ever go someplace, we all got to sit without talking 'cause you spend the whole time on your phone."

"Mom, Jalen and I can go out if you just want to stay home and chill," Melissa said.

"Melissa. That's not very polite at all," Kathleen said in my defense.

I just stood there again for a moment realizing that Avery had constructed some pretty serious walls with these two children. Okay, so maybe I didn't have any children in my other life, but, even so, I figured I could do a better job than Avery Douglas had done.

"Okay," I said, interchangeably looking at Melissa and Jalen. "You two come up with a place to go to and I agree to turn my phone off while we sit at dinner."

Initially, the kids stared at me as if I were an alien from another galaxy. Kathleen actually had a tear in each eye as she smiled broadly.

"Cool," Melissa blurted out. "That's a deal."

Within minutes, Melissa and Jalen had the restaurant picked out and we were in Kathleen's current year Lincoln Navigator SUV and headed out to dinner as a family. As she drove to our location, Kathleen reached over to the passenger seat and held my hand. I was amazed to think just how little it took to really make this beautiful woman happy.

During our dinner together, I opened up conversation about Melissa'a dancing and Jalen's ball playing. I asked Melissa what her favorite dances were, which ones were the most difficult for her, and a wide assortment of questions. The girl lit up like a

Christmas tree. She was elated when I promised to attend her next dance recital.

Jalen, being younger, was not as conversant, but I did get him to talk a bit about baseball and I hit a home run with him when I promised to take him to the batting cages.

I ordered a steak for my dinner and Kathleen appeared a bit perplexed when I informed the server that I wanted my steak cooked medium well.

"Well, that's a first," she said. "I've never known you to order a steak any way but rare."

Kathleen also seemed surprised when I made an ugly face and the kids giggled when I said that I did not like mushrooms.

Throughout the evening, we laughed, talked, and, quite frankly, I never heard Melissa chat that much in all the time I had been around her.

True to my word, I kept my phone turned off, which actually turned out to be a plus when I discovered later that my mysterious female admirer had called me that evening.

It's definitely an odd feeling when you see a person for the very first time in your life and have to pretend that you've known each other for years. That's how it was when Stan came by and picked me up at our home the next morning. He seemed to be a rather gregarious guy and at a pudgy five feet eight inches, with a bulbous nose, a frock of very curly brown hair, and full lips, he even looked the part.

Kathleen greeted him at the door and it was apparent that they at least knew one another, as she asked him how Sylvia and the kids were doing. Of course, that helped me a bit, as I now knew that Stan's wife was named Sylvia and he apparently had children. It struck me once again that I not only lived amidst a barrage of lies and falsities, but I constantly had to tread on thin ice, careful never to reveal that I did not know things that a true Avery Douglas should know.

The ride to the office was pleasant. Stan pulled into a covered parking lot, parked in spot number 109, and mentioned how 110 continued to appear so empty ever since I was injured. He led me to the elevators. The eleventh floor was where the offices of Armstrong, Baldwin & Vaughn, Financial Advisors were located. I watched as he passed his card in front of a reader that gave us access to the offices. I recalled having a card like that in my wallet. As we entered, Stan looked over towards the security system and laughed.

"Came in here when the office was closed up about a month or so ago. Had to pick up something. The damn security system was armed. Two Mantles, a Ruth, and a Maris," he said. "Only way I ever can remember numbers is to link them. Guess I'll always bleed Yankee blue."

Before I could even comment, if there was a comment to be made, Stan said something that startled me.

"You know, Avery, the way you're performing around here, folks say they wouldn't be surprised if we become known as Armstrong, Baldwin, Vaughn & Douglas before too long."

I simply smiled, shrugged, and couldn't wait to change the subject since I had no freaking idea what I purportedly did for a living and why I was apparently so successful at it.

The first person to greet me was a super attractive young lady with platinum hair that extended past her shoulders and a skirt that was far short of her knees, sitting at the front reception desk. I was very thankful for the nameplate on her desk that informed me that her name was Jamie Glover.

As Stan led me further into the office, we bypassed an area where people were seated either openly at desks or in booths and entered an area of private offices.

"Ed Farley should be in today," Stan said and, within minutes, we were standing at the entrance to an office where Farley was seated at his desk. We exchanged greetings and questions about my well-being before we moved on. I also quickly encountered Sid Logan and Lois Mandarin.

I had three "saving graces" on that day. I had Stan guiding me. I had the fact that private offices all bore name plates outside the door revealing whose office it was, and, finally, I had a day when a number of the broker/agents were not actually in the office. This meant that my chances of making a mistake in a discussion with someone were greatly reduced.

As we entered yet another segment of the offices, I immediately noticed that my office and Stan's were in a section where the offices were larger, the furnishings more exquisite, and the section itself was sequestered from other areas. I correctly surmised that people such as Stan and myself were at a higher level than others—likely just a notch below people such as Armstrong, Baldwin, and Vaughn, if they even existed or were still among the living. The door to my office was closed. I spotted the reader, pulled the access card from my wallet, and used it to unlock the door. I correctly assumed that my card was keyed to open the office outer door and the door to my private office.

As I entered the plush room, Stan assured me that whenever I was ready to head home, he would gladly transport me back. I stood there in awe for a moment, taking in the exquisite surroundings that comprised my office.

A drop-dead-gorgeous brunette poked her head in while Stan was still with me. She ran up to me, gave me a big hug, and smiled profusely. She told me how good it was to see me again, how glad she was that I was on the mend, and how available she was if I needed anything. Once again, Stan, even without his realizing it, came to my rescue.

"Marilyn has been holding down the fort on your accounts in your absence," Stan said, "and helping me make sure we don't miss anything. Don't know what we'd do without her."

I smiled. Thanked her. Thanked Stan, also. And I listened closely to Marilyn's voice to see if I could detect whether she was the mysterious female who had been calling me. I quickly surmised that she did not seem to be that person.

As I sat alone for a moment at my desk, admiring the number of awards that graced the walls of my office and the exquisite desk, chairs, and furnishings, I reflected upon what I had learned so far during my office visit. My immediate assessment was that I had actually grasped nothing other than what Stan and a few of the office workers looked like, the fact that some great looking females worked here, and that this woman named, Marilyn, somehow directly assisted Stan and me. Most importantly, I did not know where to begin in trying to figure out whether my work and the threatening phone call were related. Nothing at my desk appeared to help. I had a computer, but did not know the password needed to utilize it. Only one of my desk drawers was locked and I did not know where the key was. Nothing else in any of the unlocked desk drawers revealed anything, except I was apparently fond of a particular brand of breath mints.

As I sat there pondering these things, Stan tapped lightly on my open door and walked in.

"Hey, man. Just a quick heads up. Ran into George Armstrong in the executive men's room. Said he heard you were in. He's headed here to stop in to see you."

Well, that seemed to answer my question as to whether there was a living icon named Armstrong anywhere within the firm that bore the name. Within minutes, that confirmation was strengthened even more when a distinguished man, whom I guesstimated to be easily in his sixth decade of life, appeared at my office door. I had to assume that I was in the presence of George Armstrong.

I started to rise when he moved quickly towards me and insisted that I remain seated as he extended his hand.

"Avery, my boy, good to see you again. I assume you're doing everything your doctors are telling you to do to assure that you'll be fully recovered?"

"Yes, sir," I responded with a smile that I hoped sent a message that I was glad to see this man again, despite the fact that I clearly had never seen him before in my life.

"Good to hear, son, we want and need you back in the trenches here."

After George Armstrong left, I sat staring out at nothing. The man who showed up next, neither knocked, nor smiled. He walked quickly into my office, while closing the door behind him. Without an advanced warning from Stan, a name tag on the guy's chest, or any other such assistance, I had no earthy idea who this man standing in my office was. I pegged this guy to be somewhere in his late 50s. He was close to six feet in height, had a slim build, an angular face with a sharply pointed nose, deeply set eyes, and gray wavy hair. My initial impression was that, if you put a moustache and goatee on his face and two short horns atop his head, he would clearly look like someone who had come from a place down under—and I'm not referring to Australia or New Zealand. A quick glance at the suit he was wearing and the jewelry that he wore also provided the distinct impression that this guy was somebody important around here.

In any event, the dude walked closer to my desk, which I immediately sensed, along with the closed door, permitted him to speak in a quieter voice and be heard only by me.

"Listen here, Avery, I'm having a really difficult time keeping Piscatulli and his boys at bay. Have you heard from them at all?"

Okay, so I had no idea who this guy standing in my office was, no idea who someone named Piscatulli was, and no idea why the tone of this man's voice was a mixture of urgency and high-level nervousness. The only thing I did know is that if I answered his question in the affirmative, I would have to provide more detail. I stared outwardly and answered.

"No. I haven't heard from anyone."

The man actually reached into his pocket, wiped his brow with a handkerchief, and pointed at finger at me.

"I don't need to tell you, Douglas, don't play with these guys. I don't care how big the bump on your head was, these are guys you don't mess around with. Take care of things, Avery, and do it fast. You hear?"

My mind was racing. I wished that I could use this opportunity to find out more, but I couldn't find a way to do so. What would I ask? Who's Piscatulli? What does he want from me? Is he a guy who either himself or through one of his associates would threaten me and my family? Oh, and, by the way, who are you?

Nothing seemed to fit, so I simply looked up at this Lucifer look-alike and nodded.

"Yeah, I hear you," I said.

I stared after him as he opened my office door and walked away.

Chapter Six

It's Getting Hotter

W hen Stan came to my office, he saw the perspiration on my brow and the paleness of my face. I am sure that he attributed that to the fact that I was recovering from a traumatic head injury, rather than that I just had a scare that had me reeling. He did inadvertently help me, once again, when he spoke to me as he was driving me back home.

"So, Marilyn tells me Artie Vaughn paid you a visit also today. Not bad. Step back in the office for the first time in a while and two of the firm's namesake icons pay you a personal visit. Guess that's what happens when you're a big cheese who brings in a whole lot of dough that helps to pad year-end bonuses, eh?"

I mumbled something, combined with a fake half-hearted chuckle, then quickly recovered enough to change the subject by thanking Stan for his babysitting role on this day.

"Hey, man, more than glad to help," Stan said. "Anytime, Avery. Just let me know if you need anything."

The more I was around Stan, the clearer it became that Avery Douglas was not a particularly nice guy, but Stan Fredrickson was just that. I was convinced that

Stan was not privy to whatever Arthur Vaughn was referring to when he came to my office. Otherwise, Vaughn would surely have relied upon Stan to take care of everything in my absence. This was especially likely, since Stan and Marilyn were overseeing my company accounts.

I returned home to a smiling Kathleen asking how my day went, while she scurried about getting ready to pick Melissa up at her dance classes. I was glad that Kathleen would be gone for a while, as I just needed some time to sit and think. I also wanted to get on the computer and see if I could pull up anything about someone named Piscatulli. If I was feeling unnerved and upset before I began surfing the web, my discomfort was greatly compounded once I began to learn more about Antonio Sylvester Piscatulli.

The reports were filled with times when the man was a person of interest in several homicides and other criminal matters. He was the defendant in one criminal trial that resulted in an acquittal. The man purportedly made his millions through an incredible number of car dealerships, but no one really bought into that story. He was perceived to be a racketeer, a felon, a gangster, and a reputed murderer. A number of people, who had crosswise dealings with Tony Piscatulli, ended up mysteriously missing or dead. But the man was as slippery as an icy mountain slope. If there was one thing that was clear when it came to Antonio Piscatulli, it was that he was a man that you would never want to be on the wrong side of in any dealings whatsoever.

I sat limply at the computer and could not shake the thought that I knew exactly where I, as Avery

Douglas, was—on the wrong side of this notorious thug.

As I lay in bed that night with my eyes wide open and my heart pounding in my chest, I spent hours agonizing over what I should do. I felt so helpless. I had nowhere to turn, no one I could trust.

I was tired of this entire charade. I never asked to be Avery Douglas and felt completely trapped. If you don't know how you ever got into something, how can you know how to get out?

I tried to convince myself that if I ran away, I might be able to spare Kathleen and the kids from harm, but I continually ended up at the same point. If I disappear, Kathleen and the children would be the only leverage that Piscatulli and his thugs would have. No way they would leave them alone. Besides, I could not help but believe that there was nowhere I could go before these guys would find me anyway.

I was doomed. I felt so empty. For the first time since this whole thing happened to me, I wished above all else that I had died in that car accident.

The next day, the children would be at school and Kathleen was going shopping with Allison Martin, a friend whose daughter, Chelsea, was in the same class at school with Melissa. The guys at the car dealership had called to ask me if they could come by and pick up the Lamborghini Aventador to service it. I offered to bring the car in. I just needed to get out a bit and find something to do to keep myself busy.

Premier Luxury Vehicles looked to be far too clean and upscale to have anything at all to do with cars. But, sure enough, I was greeted by none other than André. He looked more like a hair stylist than a guy working at an auto dealership.

I agreed to sit in the plush waiting room, while they serviced the car. As I sat alone, drinking my cappuccino and eating a few Belgium imported cookies, a tall man, wearing a navy blue pinstriped suit, a red tie, and dark sunglasses, came in and sat next to me. At first, he merely nodded his head in greeting, picked up a magazine, started reading, and sat quietly. Then, without lifting his head or eyes from the magazine or looking at me, he pulled something from his pocket with one hand and faced it towards me. I had never before seen FBI credentials, but that was what they purported to be.

"Morning, Mr. Douglas. I am Special Agent Stephen Sundberry, FBI. Please just remain calm. I'd like to take a moment to chat with you without causing a fuss or drawing any unwarranted attention."

A bolt of fear, combined with shock, raced through my body. I said nothing.

"I would think that a man such as yourself would have some familiarity with the criminal penalties for engaging in money laundering and the dictates of RICO, The Racketeer Influenced and Corrupt Organizations Act, that provides extended criminal penalties for acts performed in concert with an ongoing criminal organization. But, as they say, Mr. Douglas, sometimes the federal government is willing to bend a bit when there are bigger fish in the pond."

I was trembling and desperately attempting to mask the extent of my fear. I said a few stupid things that I reflected back on afterwards.

"I ... uh ... I'm afraid I have no idea what you're talking about. You must have the wrong guy."

"Listen, Douglas, we've been tracking your dealings with the likes of Antonio Piscatulli for a while now. We've got more than enough to hang you and a few of your colleagues out to dry."

Now, for the first time, he turned his head towards me, momentarily lifted his sunglasses from his eyes, and stared into mine.

"These are not mere threats, Mr. Douglas, they are facts. The only reason I don't cuff you right now, arrest you, and escort you out of here is because we're interested in your cooperation in assisting us with Piscatulli. You give us what we need and we can make life a whole lot more tolerable for you and your family. I can't promise you there will be no consequences for your criminal acts, but your cooperation will go a long way in shortening any time you will spend in a federal prison."

Then, the man stood up, handed me his card, and began to walk away.

"This is not the time nor place for the type of extended conversation we need to have. You can contact me at any time. I will also be back in touch with you. My advice is that you speak to no one else about this and think real hard at what's at stake."

He walked out of the room and was gone, leaving me even more of a basket case than I was before he ever made his surprise appearance.

Well, at least I had my answer. The threatening call I received was most likely one of Piscatulli's cohorts. I somehow was involved in cleaning up "dirty money" on behalf of a big-time mobster who was heavily in the sights of the Federal Bureau of Investigation.

And, the greatest irony of all was that, in addition to the awareness I had of what this man would do to me if he ever caught scent that I was cooperating with the feds, I honestly could not cooperate. They would want names, facts, stats, data, events and I had absolutely none of that. If by tomorrow I agreed to cooperate fully with the FBI, it would take them about thirty seconds before they determined that I was stringing them along. I had nothing to give.

I drove back home in the Lamborghini, shaking all the way. I felt sick to my stomach. Surely, I could try to convince the world's most powerful law enforcement agency that I was not really Avery Douglas and that I believed he was somehow tucked away in my comatose body in a hospital in another state some 1,800 miles away. Yeah, that might work. I mean who wouldn't believe that? These federal agents likely have heard every excuse and claim of innocence possible. Mine would certainly rank way up there among the most popular to be discussed in the office break room. It would not merely be a claim that they had the wrong guy. It would be a claim that they had the right guy, but the wrong physical body. Now that's certainly a classic.

Even before I got back home, my cell phone buzzed. I grabbed it quickly without even looking at the screen, expecting it to be Kathleen.

"Heard you had a visitor today," the voice said. "The Man, he doesn't like that kind of news. Gets him very upset, you know? People think they can sell him out by cutting a better deal with the feds."

"Hey," I responded. "I didn't say a word to anybody and don't intend to. He ... uh ... the guy came to me. I had no idea he would show up like that. D-don't even know how he knew I was there."

"Oh, they know. Just like we know things."

"Look, I'm telling you. I don't have anything to say to anybody. You tell that to the boss. I have nothing to say."

"Hahaha. I'll be sure to tell him that. He likes that kind of news. Besides, guys tried to cut deals with the feds in the past. It didn't work. The boss, he ain't living locked up nowhere. He's got a big beautiful home, nice big pool, and all."

I remained silent and the caller did also. For a moment, I thought maybe we'd been disconnected or he had hung up, but I glanced quickly at the screen and saw that the call was still live. Then, he spoke again.

"You know, they can promise you a shorter time in the pen, but that lovely wife of yours and them kids still gonna be out there somewhere. Never forget that."

Then, he did hang up.

Chapter Seven

Gotta Get Proactive

I was sitting in the study still struggling greatly with what my next move should be when I came across something of interest that I had never noticed before. Avery's desk had a secret compartment. I stumbled upon it accidentally. When I did, I was so shocked that I immediately rose up from the chair and closed the door to room. I had to. I felt as if I was about to look through things that were very private and very significant to my survival. Let's face it. By now, I knew at least enough about Avery Douglas to assume that, if he had anything hidden away in a secret compartment in his desk, it likely had to do with one of two things— secret women in his life and secret wrongful money dealings. I was about to learn that I was one hundred percent right on both counts.

The first thing I pulled out was Avery's little black book. Huh? People really have such a thing? Well, Avery certainly did. He had a list of names, phone numbers, and detailed accounts with dates when he was apparently with different women. At first glance, I assumed that he kept these details as a kind of trophy case, but after perusing through things a bit, I sensed something far more nefarious. He had details on wealthy socialite women with whom he had been involved. These were women he was in a position to blackmail, if need be. I determined this when I saw the names of some of the husbands of the women listed. They were men of position, power, influence, and wealth. Seemed as if all I ever did was turn up one rock after another to discover a new low-life aspect of this man's personality. When it came to being in another person's identity, I seemed to have found a way to scrape the very bottom of the barrel.

I put the black book down and picked up a small ledger. My hands shook as I flipped through the pages. There were dates and references to large sums of money. There were many shorthand symbols and codes that I did not understand, but enough that I did. One of the more prominent names was A.P., which I surmised could be Antonio Piscatulli. Large numbers preceded by dollar signs made me think that folks smarter than me would likely understand the recorded transactions that Avery Douglas was citing in his records. There was much that made no sense to me, but the initials A.V. made me think of Arthur Vaughn. References to "The Sen," and "Judge" sent chills through my body. Mention of "Max L" brought to mind a local millionaire named Maximillian Lederer, who owned two professional franchises. Still, even with all these references, I was merely guessing.

I thought I had discovered everything useful until I saw a reference to Avery's email address followed by "Marville779." I had no idea what that meant, but it sure looked like a password to me. So, I booted up the desktop computer, typed in Avery's email address, and took a shot at Marville779. Bingo! Just like that, I was in. I began to search everything. Email messages, files, software programs, everything and anything that I could search with my limited forensic computer skills.

Okay, so based upon a few emails, I had likely discovered that the name of my mysterious phone call lover was Ramona, but, beyond that, I did not uncover a whole lot more. I wondered if Avery used the same password at work that he was using on his personal computer. I had to know. If there was more incriminating evidence on his computer at work, I needed to find it. If I were to approach the authorities, I could not do so as someone who knew about the illegal doings of Avery Douglas. I had to know enough under the guise that I was Avery Douglas and everything and anything I surrendered would be from first-hand knowledge. I now knew what I had to do next.

"Just out," I said to Kathleen when she inquired as to where I was going at night. "That's all you need to know, so get off my back and let it go."

I could see the hurt on her face. It was the first time I had ever been harsh with her, but I readily surmised that it was something she had encountered many times through the years from the real Avery. So, perhaps lately, since I had assumed Douglas' identity, Kathleen had begun to hope that a knock on the head had helped to give her a kinder, less-of-a-tyrant-husband. I was sorry to destroy any such hope she might have been harboring, but I had to get away. Little did Kathleen know that I was actually fighting to protect her and the children.

I had always been very good with directions. It did not matter anyway, since I punched in the address to the office in the GPS and drove away. When I pulled into the parking lot, I considered parking in spot number 110 which I believed was my own designated spot based upon the comment made by Stan, but thought better of it. I chose a spot on the floor above the one Stan had parked at and headed for that same elevator we had ridden. When I reached the eleventh floor, I placed my access card in front of the reader and smiled as the door opened. A buzzing sound startled me and sent a warning that the security system was set and I did not know the four-digit code. The beeping was getting faster and faster and I knew the alarm was getting ready to go off. My hands were clammy. I punched in 1-2-3-4, but those numbers were clearly not the correct code. Man, I hadn't even thought of a security system. This was the last thing I needed. I considered just aborting my plan and getting out of there, when I recalled Stan's seemingly inane comment when we had entered the offices.

"Two Mantles, a Ruth, and a Maris," he had said. "Well, I may have been living in Minnesota and rooting for the Twins, but, thankfully, I knew a whole lot about the Yankees from my dad, who grew up in the Bronx. And he once took me to the old Yankee Stadium and we visited Monument Park.

I quickly punched in 7-7-3-9, based upon the jersey numbers worn by Mantle, Ruth, and Maris. As I did, the beeping stopped. I sighed deeply and wiped the perspiration from my face. I wasn't sure who I was more thankful for, dad and his love for the Bronx Bombers or Stan and his comment when we entered the offices. Guess I owed both of them for this one.

I left all the office lights turned off as I wended through the darkened offices towards my office. When I got there, I once again used my access card to unlock the door.

I booted up the computer that sat on the desk and hoped for the best. Man, I was on a roll today. The same password did give me access to Avery's office computer. Now, as I searched around, I found some files that I could not access. I attempted to utilize the same password, but this time it did not work—so much for my roll.

I honestly did not know enough about Avery Douglas to start guessing at other passwords, so I simply did the next best thing. I realized that people generally do not want to create a myriad of other passwords, so they will often either use the same password or a variation of it. Instead of Marville779, I tried 977, then 797, then 780. Nothing was working. I don't know just what made me think of it, but I decided to simply change the first word. I entered Narville779, not really expecting much. I gasped as that password opened the file. I quickly placed a flash drive I had brought with me from home and began to copy everything. I knew I had struck oil or something of value when I saw much more factual and data detail and initials were replaced with actual names. The names Antonio Piscatulli, Senator Harold Fischer, Judge William Goldblatt, and Maximillian Lederer were all spelled out and further identified with dates and dollar amounts. But, something even more revealing was delineated. Antonio Piscatulli was identified as "Biscayne Enterprises, CEO, William Schaefer." In each case, the actual individual was apparently entered in the company books by a corporate and individual name different that differed from the person's actual name.

So, that told me several things. It was possible, even likely, that not everyone in Armstrong, Baldwin & Vaughn had any idea that they had people such as

Piscatulli, Harold Fischer, Goldblatt, and Lederer as clients. That very likely meant that no one was supposed to know that. Avery Douglas was laundering money for these folks and investing ill-gotten funds into some package or another to help make them look clean and legit.

As I was copying everything onto the flash drive, I did not know what all of this would mean to me personally, but I believed that I now had at least something to give to the feds that might help me to bargain for safe protection for Kathleen and the children.

I was still very scared, still very confused, but I actually smiled as I sat waiting for the computer to transfer everything onto the flash drive.

My smile quickly disappeared when I heard someone entering the office at the front door.

Chapter Eight

Back at the Office

I scurried towards the front of the office, close enough where I could at least hear what was going on. It sounded to me as if more than one person was entering. I could hear their voices, but could not make out what they were saying. Then, I heard someone punching a code into the security alarm system. They must have assumed the alarm was triggered and did not even realize that it was turned off. Now, when they would look at it, they would see that it was disarmed. From a distance, I could see flashlights sending out beams in advance of whomever had entered. I was sure that people who worked here did not come in with flashlights.

I ran back to my office hoping above all else that the flash drive had captured everything I needed. It had and I quickly detached it from the computer, shoved it in my pocket, and shut the computer down. I was so frightened that my legs seemed paralyzed. I had to get out of there, but I had no idea where I should or even could go. I didn't know the logistics of this facility. I had only been here once before, even though I supposedly worked here. Plus, I didn't have a flashlight and the hallways here were much too dark to navigate quickly.

All of this would be fine if I were James Bond or Jason Bourne or even that Kent Taylor guy from the "Nowhere Trilogy" of books that I read. But I'm not any of those people. In fact, I'm not even Avery Douglas. What in the world was I thinking when I decided to do this tonight?

I considered that maybe I should just let these guys see me. They're probably some of Piscatulli's thugs. I could just tell them I came in to check things out on my own computer and was going to start deleting some records when I heard them coming and was frightened. Yeah, that'll work. They'll believe that. Makes perfect sense that I had to sneak into my own office at night in the dark in order to access my own records and never got to delete them anyway. I mean that sounds pretty normal. Doesn't it?

Of course, maybe they'll search me and find the flash drive containing all sorts of data that I claimed I came here to delete. Who am I kidding? These guys probably want to clear out my computer before they find a way to dispose of me. I had the frightening thought that finding me here tonight might help them to kill the proverbial two birds with one stone. That's a pretty stupid saying, anyway. Nobody kills two birds with one stone and thinking of killing, at a time like this, was the very last thing that I needed to be doing, anyway.

No, I knew what I needed to do. I had to find a way to get out of here and stay alive. I also needed to find ways to assure that Kathleen and the children would be safe.

As I tiptoed out of my office, I closed the door and scurried away. The hallway turned at that point. If these two guys stopped at my office, I would be temporarily safe. If they did not, I was in big trouble.

Beyond me, there was one more set of doors. I remembered that when George Armstrong left my office, he headed to the left in the direction that I had done now. Stan's office and mine were separated by a small conference room. I knew that. But, there were not enough offices for Armstrong, Baldwin, and Vaughn, the big three, unless they were in an area beyond those two doors just ahead of me. I was also convinced that there was nothing beyond the offices of George Armstrong, Harold Baldwin, and Arthur Vaughn. If I got caught here, I would be a cornered rat and we all know what people generally do once they corner a rat.

As I, very carefully, peered around the corner, I could see the beams from the flashlights bouncing off the walls and the floor. My hands were clammy. My lips and chin were trembling. Once again, I felt dizzy with a weakness in my legs and knees. My chest started to hurt. I momentarily considered that my way out of this might be the heart attack I was threatening to have. I've watched a bunch of movies where some hero is in a position similar to mine and they handle it with incredible poise and calmness. I can't speak for everyone, but what I was experiencing wasn't even in the same ballpark of those dudes. For me, victory would be realized if I did not vomit, faint, or drop dead within the next few minutes or so.

I quickly spotted two men. One was burly, built like a Mack truck. All I could see was outlines and shadows of these two individuals. The angle of Mr. Mack Truck's flashlight provided me with a slightly better view of the other man. He was taller and much thinner. As he turned his head, I detected that he wore glasses and had long curly hair that was as unkempt as the hair on his face. It seemed to me that one guy was the enforcer, the other was the computer geek.

"Okay, stop here. This is the one," I heard one of the men say as they stood outside my office with a light shining on my nameplate. I quickly realized that it was computer geek doing the talking. "This is the office we need to access. The security card we have should open the door for us."

"Well, if it don't," the big guy moved his jacket aside and patted his holstered weapon, "I can always bypass the system."

Geek did not actually laugh. He was too busy trying to position the card in front of the reader. I heard the click as the door unlocked and Mr. Burly pushed it open with his foot.

"Okay then," enforcer guy said, "let's get this done. We gonna have a hard enough time with you having to crack the dude's passwords and stuff. Do whatever you need to do. I don't wanna be here all night."

"Just be patient," computer geek said. "These things take time. Look, I'm real good at this, but even I have to work at things a bit. Just don't get me upset. I need to maintain my focus. This work is delicate, like opening a safe."

"Hell, if I wanna safe opened," burly man said, "I blast it open."

The big guy's laugh sounded like a strange combination of a donkey's bray and a chicken's cackle. Geek guy reminded me of *Star Trek's* Mr. Spock. Emotions had no existence with him. Everything was factual and his mind immediately assessed things as correct, incorrect, or undetermined.

"Well, you most certainly cannot blast open computer codes, passwords, and files. Besides, it is imperative, at this point in time, that we keep this computer alive."

Mr. Mack Truck laughed and, as he did, I once again considered that he would be a hoot in a barnyard.

"Okay, okay, the computer stays alive. But we can't say the same for the guy what owns it, eh?"

And, yet again, the big guy laughed at his own remark.

I was immediately reminded how interesting it is about what some people consider to be funny and others do not. Well, at least I had some confirmation that my "matter of life and death thoughts" were not the result of an overactive imagination on my part.

The way I had it figured, the safer choice would have been to simply wait things out, let these guys finish whatever they were doing, and then slip out afterwards. My other option would be to try to sneak by my office while they were inside. Unfortunately, I could see that they left the door open. But when you're in the position that I was, it is almost impossible to think clearly.

I decided to move as furtively as possible past the open door of my office and out the building. These men had never turned any lights on, so the hallway was still in the dark. I had to think that the two men in my office were certainly not expecting anyone to pass by the door. The geek was surely deeply entrenched in his computer forensics. Bubba was probably sitting in a chair playing some mindless game on his cell phone. All I needed to do was quietly sneak past the door, move on down the hall, and get out of this place.

And I would have made it too, if my cell phone did not start to ring just as I was walking past my office.

Chapter Nine

Beyond My Limits

I've heard people use expressions that they were so frightened something made their blood run cold. In my case, my blood temperature had to be well below freezing. I was never so frightened in my life as I was at that moment. I'm actually surprised that I somehow found the strength to run, but I did. Of course, "Joe the Cement Block" was out of the room in a flash and hot on my trail. The guy must have been a formidable football player some sixty pounds ago, because bulky or not, the dude could run. I had no idea if the Geekster was behind him somewhere and I sure as heck wasn't going to wait around to find out. And let me tell you, if I was scared a few minutes earlier, I reached a level I did not know even existed when I heard the first shot and something whizzed by my head and slammed into the wall.

When I reached the front entryway, I was sure that I would never be able to open the doors and get out before monster mash would have caught up to me. Besides, I had no idea how far one of his bullets would carry, but there was no doubt in my mind he would use me for target practice before I ever cleared the office doors. So, I did not stop at the entryway nor even attempt to exit the office. I just kept running into the dark hallway trying as hard as I could not to hyperventilate as I ran.

What was I going to do? Where could I hide? How could I possibly get away from a guy with a gun? Once the behemoth realized that I had not run out of the office, he would surely turn the lights on, get his techie buddy to help him, and eventually find me. All they really had to do was make sure I did not circle back and get out the front doors. I ran so hard, blind to whatever was in front of me, that my body was shocked when I slammed into a piece of furniture. I hoped that Avery had good knees, because I wondered if I had just broken a kneecap. I quickly surmised that a broken knee surely could not hurt more than bullets being emptied into my body, so I sucked it up and started running again. I had no time at all to accurately appraise my injuries, but I could still stand and run, so I was quite sure that nothing was broken.

Suddenly, the lights were on and I realized that my predator was no longer racing after me. He didn't need to and he knew it. He would move methodically, keeping his eyes open and his gun ready, until he eventually found me. And now, for the first time, I received the confirmation that computer guy was also on the prowl.

"Just stay to the left side over there, Edson," I heard the big guy say. "Stay nice and steady and make sure he don't get back towards them front doors."

Think, man, think. Stop with the panic stuff and think. If you intend to stay alive, you're going to have to get creative here. Come up with a plan.

Okay, so the best plan I could come up with was that, as best I knew, the geekster was not packing. I couldn't be sure, but there was a chance he did not have a gun. Secondly, if he did, he probably wasn't as skilled as his partner. I could be wrong. The computer guy could be an expert marksman who doubled as a serial killer when he wasn't working on computers. But, all in all, given what I knew, I had to figure that my best odds were against that curly haired guy with glasses.

Okay, so now, I had to come up with some kind of plan to deal with him. As I continued to run down the hall, I came upon another group of offices. These did not have nameplates outside the door or readers. I ran to the far end of the hall and reached a dead end. No emergency exit at the end of the hall. I was trapped. I had nowhere to go and I could hear my pursuers headed my way. I quickly reached over for the door handle of one of the offices. It was unlocked. So, now I was in a small office on the eleventh floor of a building. I had no way out. Even the floor to ceiling windows didn't open should I decide to leap eleven stories and hope to land in a deep swimming pool or huge fluffy mattress or something. My body was shaking. I was drenched in perspiration. I could hear doors opening and closing along the hallway as the two guys chasing me were checking each office. I have never had a clue as to how I would eventually die. But, I never imagined I would find myself waiting for a former running back and his highbrowed partner to eventually find me cowering inside an office and kill me. This never seemed to happen to the heroes on a popular television drama series or in a movie.

I paused for a moment, took a deep breath, and made a concerted effort to compose myself. I closed my eyes for a moment and, before opening them again, took a few short breaths. I would love to tell you that a deep peace came upon me, but nothing of the sort happened. When I opened my eyes again, I was as frightened and trembling as I had been just moments earlier.

The small office that I was in was dark since I did not turn the lights on. I mean that would have been like announcing to the guys chasing me not to bother checking any other offices on their way towards where I was located. Yet, despite the darkness in that room, some light crept in from under the door and some from the moon casting its nightly silvery glow through the eleventh-floor windows. That's when I spotted it. Whoever worked out of this office had a golf club, a putter, standing in a corner beside the desk. Of course, he also had one of those electronic indoor putting machines that returns the ball after you sink a putt. I didn't care one bit about the machine. I quickly grabbed the putter. It was certainly no match for a gun, but, with the element of surprise, it might just do the trick.

I positioned myself to the side of the office door so that it would open towards me and I would not immediately be seen when someone opens the door. I was holding that club so tightly that my fingers were cramping. This entire deal was preposterous. Here I was being pursued by two men who I believed would kill me once they found me and I honestly did not know whether I had ability to strike someone with a golf club, even if the opportunity did present itself. This was not my world. I had never struck someone like that in my entire life. The very thought of swinging a club as hard as I could and striking someone with it was entirely foreign to me—and frightening as all get out.

I remembered the big guy ordering geeko to stay on the left side, while he stayed on the right. The office I was in was on the left side of the hall, so I assumed that it would be data-man who would check out the office where I was hidden. Well, at least, as best I knew, the computer dude did not have a weapon. I heard the two men getting closer to me. They continued to open and close doors, so I had a strong sense as to where they were. My heart started pumping furiously as I heard the office door next to me open and the lights click on. I was next. I was an absolute wreck. Now I was not only trembling, but my hands were soaked from perspiration and I was no longer sure that I could maintain a firm grip on the club, even if I were to use it against my attacker.

Suddenly, the door opened, a hand reached in and flicked the lights on. For a fleeting moment, I spotted a tattoo. It was small, but distinct. The blade of a knife extended through what appeared to a pair of black old-fashioned handcuffs. I had seconds to make my move and surprisingly I did. I swung that club as hard as I possibly could and heard a cracking sound as my makeshift weapon came to a jarring stop upon making contact with its target. The crack I heard had to be the guy's jawbone, because the club struck him squarely in the face. I was stunned that I had actually done this. Some might attribute my actions to courage. I know that everything I did was birthed out of extreme fear. Then again, who cares what motivated me. One of my assailants was now lying unconscious on the floor of the office and imagine my added shock when I realized that it was not the computer geek. I had felled the "Incredible Hulk."

His weapon was right there next to his fallen bulk, so I picked it up. At the very least, I wanted to be sure that if he came to before I got out of there, he would no longer have a gun to shoot at me. Although, I must admit, it did not look as if this guy would be up and on his feet anytime soon.

I quickly peered my head out into the hallway to see if I could spot the techie and I quickly did. He was standing in the doorway of an office further down than mine and on the side opposite from me. I quickly learned that another of my assertions was incorrect when a bullet that he fired missed me by no more than an inch. I waited and when I saw movement I fired back, then made a run for it down the hall. I quickly ducked inside another office. He fired at me again and I returned fire. This went on for a time or two more until I was at the front entryway.

I have no idea whether he followed me out or went back to find his partner. I hit the stairway and must have set some type of speed record in covering eleven floors before entering the garage. Most of that remains a blur to me. I remember the distinct feeling that, at any moment, I would feel the pain of bullets entering my body—okay, technically, Avery's body—but that never happened. The next thing I remember, I was firing up the Lamborghini and racing out of that area while violating every speed limit around.

When I was far enough away to garner some assurance that I was not being followed or within range of gunfire, I pulled over, extracted the business card from my wallet, and punched in the number.

Chapter Ten

Already in Prison

I had no idea whether this guy would really answer his phone at night, so it did surprise me when after four rings he answered.

"Sundberry," he said. Nothing more, just his name.

My first attempt was to keep my voice steady and sound like a man who was in control of himself. When the initial words out of my mouth sounded like someone who had just sucked helium out of a balloon, I knew that I had failed miserably.

"Agent Sundberry, you said I could call you at any time, so I did. I'm calling you. I'm calling you right now. I know it's outside of, you know, outside the normal business hours and stuff, but, I needed to call now. You know? So that's why I'm calling you."

"Would you mind telling me first who you are?"

Oh yeah. I guess I just assumed he would know it was me calling.

""Uh, yeah, right, this is … uh … Avery Douglas here."

"And how can I help you, Mr. Douglas?"

"They just tried to kill me. I got away. The big dude might still be lying there on the floor after I hit him with a golf club. I have no idea where the computer guy is."

At first, Sundberry said nothing, but it soon became obvious that despite his years of experience as an FBI field agent, he could not decipher my babbling. He finally got me to slow down long enough for me to tell him that I was at my office gathering up some data that would be helpful to the FBI, when two men entered the office and I had a run-in with them.

"I'm going to send a couple of my guys over to that office now, Mr. Douglas. I want you to go straight home. I will meet you there. We'll make plans to get your wife and children out of there as quickly as possible. Can you do that, Mr. Douglas? Can you head straight home? Are you able to drive safely, sir?"

I was already breathing better. I knew that I was by no means out of danger yet, but just the fact that Sundberry was already talking about taking steps to protect Kathleen, Melissa, and Jalen helped immensely to calm me down. So, maybe I was headed for prison, but, at least, Kathleen and the kids would be safe. Heck, I was already in a form of prison anyway by being housed in the body of a man I did not like and did not want to be.

I'll say one thing for Special Agent Sundberry. The guy had used his credentials to get through the gate and was parked outside of our home, waiting in his car by the time I arrived. I later learned that he did, indeed, send a team over to the office. They could clearly see that something had occurred over there as lights were on, some furniture was knocked over, and there was some blood on a carpet in one of the smaller offices. There was no sign, however, of the two men who had come after me. The FBI guys are really slick, but I had to assume that Piscatulli's thugs also were very adept in their own right. This was especially true when they needed to clean up a mess.

Sundberry sat with me and Kathleen and pretty much educated her to the fact that her husband was a criminal and the guys threatening our family were some very dangerous dudes. He assured us that, on that very night, the FBI could have a team come in and get everyone to a temporary safe place beyond the reach of the notorious Antonio Piscatulli. Kathleen sat quietly, but, before long, tears streamed down her face.

I'll never forget the pain I felt when she turned to me and spoke.

"How could you, Avery? How could you put the lives of our children and my life at stake because of your greed? I never asked you for this house, the cars we have, nothing like that. I-I just wanted a husband that w-would love me and our children and grow old together with me. How could you?"

I was speechless. What could I possibly say?

Within hours, Kathleen, the children, and I were relocated to a safe house that even we did not know where it was located. The van that transported us had a comfortable enough interior, but no windows for us to know where we were at any point in time. Of course, it was dark when we arrived. The house seemed pleasant enough. It was located at the end of a cul-de-sac. A tall wooden fence surrounded the property.

As expected, the house was fully furnished. The layout was open and inviting with a large den area, a good-sized kitchen, Florida room at the back of the house overlooking an outdoor patio, and nicely manicured lawn. Its three bedrooms meant that Kathleen and I would share the master bedroom, while Melissa and Jalen would each have their own room. The split design had the master bedroom on one side of the house, while the two bedrooms, with a Jack and Jill bathroom between them, were situated on the other side. In addition to the master bath, there was a half bath located off the den, next to the laundry room.

"This is temporary," Sundberry had informed us, "until a more permanent arrangement can be made. You'll be safe here, plus one of our agents will be here with you at all times. The agent on duty will stay up front. Most of the time, you'll hardly know that he or she is even here."

Melissa and Jalen were initially frightened and wide-eyed when we woke them and quickly ushered them from the house. They were told there was a problem and we were temporarily under the protection of the FBI.

"It has to do with your father's work," Kathleen told the children. She omitted telling them that I was about to spend some considerable time locked up in a federal prison. I honestly believe she held back from telling them that their father was a criminal for their benefit, rather than to somehow preserve my dignity. She did a really great job appearing to be civil towards me when we were in front of the children. When we were together alone, she did not even speak to me.

Three days, we were told. We would be at this location for three days before U.S. Marshals from the United States Federal Witness Protection Program would take custody of Kathleen and the children and I would be formally arrested and taken away by the FBI.

On the second day that we were at the safe house, Special Agent Stephen Sundberry arrived with a federal marshal named Rachel Scarletta and spoke to Kathleen and me.

"The United States Federal Witness Protection Program," Sundberry said, "is also known as the 'Witness Security Program.' It's administered by the United States Department of Justice and operated by the United States Marshals Service."

"Our entire goal," Rachel Scarletta said, "is to assure that you and your children are protected."

Scarletta observed closely as Kathleen continued to twist her rings, shift her position in an effort to get comfortable, and blow out a series of short breaths in an effort to somehow gain control of herself.

"Since this program began in 1971, Mrs. Douglas," Scarletta said, "we have protected, relocated, and given new identities to nearly ten thousand family members of a witness."

"Your husband is being criminally charged, Mrs. Douglas," Sundberry said. "We want to be completely honest with you. But, his willingness to come forward and work with us is paying off in some big dividends for you and your children."

"Right," Scarletta said. "You, your daughter, and your son, will be placed under our full protection. No Witness Security Program participant has ever been harmed or killed while under the active protection of the U.S. Marshals Service. As long as you follow the program guidelines, you and your children will be completely safe."

That evening, the children were already asleep, while Kathleen was sitting alone on the backyard patio. I approached her.

"Listen, after tomorrow, I will be completely out of your life. I am asking for you to give me just a few minutes to talk with you. Tomorrow will be a busy day as the Marshals come to take you, Melissa, and Jalen away."

Kathleen did not respond to me. In fact, she would not even look at me. But I figured that if she was not going to grant my request, she would have clearly told me to go away. I pulled a chair next to her and spoke.

"I know this isn't going to be easy for you and the children, Kathleen, but all three of you are young enough to press on and find a new life. I hope that somehow you will believe that you are a wonderful mother, a wonderful person, and you deserve only the very best in life.

Silent tears fell from Kathleen's eyes as she turned and finally looked at me. If there was a way to see inside the heart and soul of another person, I was sure that I would see the depth of hurt and betrayal that Kathleen was feeling. She stunned me with her next words.

"I reached a point where I pretended that I didn't know about the constant philandering, Avery, but I did know. Our marriage had already grown cold, but I wanted so desperately to keep things intact and stable for Melissa and Jalen.

Why? Why, in addition to years of ignoring me and never having any quality time for the children, did you also have to be a liar and a thief? What happened to you? Did you ever really love me? Or was I simply your 'trophy wife'?"

As the tears poured from her face, a dam burst within me. If I was going to rot away in a prison cell for crimes I did not commit, I thought that the only satisfaction I needed was to know that this precious woman and those two innocent children would all be safe and protected. Suddenly that wasn't enough. I couldn't leave things this way. I had to tell her. Even if she would never believe me, I wanted her to know.

Until now, everything I had done was for Kathleen and the children. This was my one moment.

Chapter Eleven

Imagine This

I remembered a quote made by Albert Einstein that floored me when I first heard it. I mean the name Einstein is synonymous with the word genius. The man was brilliant. Yet, he was quoted as saying that there was something even more important than knowledge and that something is the human imagination. Okay, so I was not about to talk about physics, relativity, or the philosophy of science, but surely I could find a way to challenge Kathleen to stretch her imagination and believe me. Then again, if I failed, I had nothing to lose.

I turned towards Kathleen. I reached over and took her hands in mine. She started to pull her arms back. I held tightly, despite not wanting to force her to do anything. As I stared into her eyes, I was once again reminded just how beautiful this woman was. But now, after having been around her for a period of time, I had come to realize that she possessed an inner beauty that, incredible as it seemed, surpassed her physical appearance.

"Kathleen, what I am about to tell you now defies logic. It is almost impossible to believe. In fact, I would not believe it myself if it had not actually happened to me."

Her furrowed brow and blank stare assured me that she honestly didn't know what to expect. The tilting of her head to the side combined with leaning her body forward gave me some hope that I, at least, had her attention.

"I tried to tell you back then. I tried to tell everyone that I am not Avery Douglas. I know, I know, Kathleen, I'm aware that what I'm saying sounds crazy. I mean, it sounds nuts to me. I can't explain it. I just know that it happened.

My name is Jeff Norman. I live in Minnesota. I had an accident and suffered a severe head injury the very night that Avery had his accident. For all I know, we had our car wrecks at the same time.

Look, all I know is that I'm not and have never been your husband. I have every reason to believe that Avery Douglas is in a hospital in Minnesota, lying in ICU in a coma, inside my body, while I am here in his."

At first, Kathleen never said a word. She just sat there and stared at me. For all I knew, she might be thinking that I was building up a case for my insanity plea at a criminal trial.

I went on telling her everything I could think of, in my effort to convince her that I was not Avery Douglas. She did not pull away nor challenge me. She simply sat there in silence.

"Until my eyes opened that day in the hospital, I had never seen you before in my life. Nor had I ever seen Melissa and Jalen."

Finally, after what seemed like an eternity of silence, Kathleen spoke.

"I want to ask you something. If you're not my husband, Avery, as you claim, once you realized that this mobster and his thugs were after you, why didn't you just run away, disappear?"

Now, for the first time since I had begun speaking with Kathleen, I began to choke up. I was having difficulty in speaking. I sighed deeply, did whatever I could think of to regain control, and compose myself.

"I could never leave you and the children exposed to this Piscatulli guy and his mobsters, Kathleen. They would use you all for leverage. I-I just couldn't do that. But, I was stuck between a rock and a hard place. If I left you and the kids behind, I was convinced these gangsters would make their move against you. I-I could never do that."

I could see tears in Kathleen's eyes. I had no idea what they actually meant, but, at least, I knew she was in some way being affected by what I was sharing with her.

"But the other problem I had was that I honestly had no idea what transpired between Avery and this Piscatulli guy. I had nothing, absolutely nothing, to give to the feds. I had to come up with something in order to be in a position to bargain with them for your protection and the children. If I gave them nothing, they would give me nothing in return.

That's why I went to the office and you heard me relate the story again to Agent Sundberry. Two of Piscatulli's guys came in while I was there and things got real interesting."

I reached into my pocket and handed a slip of paper to Kathleen. On it, I had written my true name, my address in Minnesota, and the hospital where someone named Jeff Norman was presently in a coma. Kathleen took the piece of paper, but, once again, said nothing.

I wiped the tears from my eyes and fought to compose myself.

"Thank you for at least listening to me, Kathleen. I realize that you may never be able to believe a word I have spoken, but, I just can't tell you how much I appreciate that you would at least listen to me. Now you know why I always avoided ever kissing you or holding you in my arms, even though I wanted to so badly. But ... but I want you to know, Kathleen, in another time and another place, I would love you with every fiber of my being."

The tears fell like crystal globules from her eyes and started to fall again from mine. I was overwhelmed with the desire to try to kiss her, but I resisted. I have no idea if she would have even permitted me to do so, but that was not the purpose of this time together. As of the next day, I would be taken away and would never see Kathleen again for the rest of my life. She would never be permitted to contact me in prison, even if she wanted to do so. Besides, I had given the flash drive of data to Sundberry and would provide some additional testimony, but I had the distinct feeling that Mr. Piscatulli would find me somewhere along the way and do his very best to assure that I never testified at any criminal trial.

I know it sounds a bit crazy, but I felt a sense of peace and fulfillment that I had this opportunity to speak honestly with Kathleen. I was quite sure that she would never believe a word I had said to her, but it mattered to me that she would hear me say that my recent activities were all geared towards finding some way to protect her, Melissa, and Jalen. Okay, so this would surely sound self-serving, but I felt particularly good that I knew in my heart I had fought for the safety of "my family." I didn't create the danger they were in, but I did help create the safety net. That felt good.

Nothing more was said between Kathleen and me that night. I slept, wearing a pair of jeans and a t-shirt, in the same bed as her—not because I wanted to, not because I am some kind of noble knight in shining armor. As far as Kathleen was concerned, I was the womanizing, lying, cheating, felon-to-be who had put the lives of my wife and children in serious jeopardy. How could I possibly expect that she would believe there was anything honorable in me? I mean, I get that. I honestly do.

We were told that the federal marshals would arrive around 9:00 a.m. to take Kathleen and the kids away. I would be taken by FBI agents, arrested, processed, and ready to undergo an extensive interrogation process. Fun, fun!

I was up early that next morning. I made myself some coffee, acknowledged the FBI agent on duty, whom I had never before seen, and prepared myself for what would be a very eventful day. As I rummaged around the kitchen, I quickly spotted two men seated in the back yard, having a smoke and chatting. I wondered if they were federal marshals or Bureau agents. Then, I spotted something that shot a bolt of fear through me. I knocked over a saucer and almost dropped the coffee mug I had been holding.

"You okay over there, man?" the agent at the front of the house asked.

I quickly sucked in some air before responding.

"Yeah, no prob. Just have butterfingers this morning. I'm going to get the kids up so they can start getting ready."

"Good idea," the agent responded. "We've got two more Bureau agents here already. The marshals should be here soon."

He shrugged and turned his attention back towards the front of the house.

I went to each of the kid's bedrooms, woke them up, and told them to quickly dress. Then, I ushered them back into the master bedroom, where Kathleen was awake, but still lying in bed. I walked over towards Kathleen and whispered in her ear.

"Something's wrong this morning, Kathleen. I don't know what it is, but I've got this crazy feeling that the wrong people are here in this house with us."

Kathleen appeared to be petrified. I gathered the kids together with Kathleen. I was extremely careful in what I said to them. I did not want to spook them.

"Listen you two. I'm not entirely comfortable with things this morning, so I want us to have a kind of emergency plan in place. The federal marshals should be here any minute, so we might be just fine, but, just in case, here's our Plan B.

I will find a way to distract everyone, while you guys all climb out of this bedroom window and get as far away from here as possible. Mom will be with you, so you have nothing to be afraid of."

"Daddy, daddy, what are you going to do?" Melissa said.

"Hey," I turned quickly towards her and placed my hands on her shoulders.

"Don't you worry about me. I'm gonna be just fine," I lied.

"I just need you guys to concentrate on what I told you to do."

Then, I did something I had not done since the day I first encountered Melissa and Jalen. I took each of them into my arms, hugged them tightly, and kissed their faces.

"Don't be afraid," I said. "Everything is going to be alright."

If I was right and these guys were not federal agents, we'd have to see how things played out once the marshals arrived. Maybe the guys in the house would let Kathleen and the kids leave, then deal with me. At least, I hoped that was true.

My heart was pumping almost out of control. A myriad of thoughts filled my mind.

How did they ever find us here? Then it struck me with the force of a tornado. Stephen Sundberry—all along, I simply assumed the guy was with the FBI because he told me he was and showed me some kind of credentials. Even when I called him, I called his cell phone. I never went through an official Bureau network to reach him. That must be it. The guy was with Piscatulli. He was a backup, intended to get me to turn over anything incriminating I had against his mob boss and I fell right into his trap. Fool. I was played. Stupid.

I didn't voice any of that to Kathleen or the kids. They were frightened enough.

I felt some relief when I spotted a van pull onto the property. I opened the bedroom door a crack as a man and woman were granted entrance to the house. The two men from the backyard were now inside.

"Federal Marshals, Silvers and Waterman," the man said, as they both showed their badges to the agents. "Our orders are to pick up the woman and two children and leave the man with you."

"Excellent, that's a roger with us," one of the agents said. "We'll get them for you. They should be ready to go. You all want some coffee or anything before you head out?"

The female marshal turned towards the man to thank him, but never got the opportunity to do so. The men moved quickly and unexpectedly lunging towards the federal marshals and slitting their throats.

I gasped as I witnessed their lifeless bodies fall to the floor.

Chapter Twelve

Minutes Turn into Seconds

I knew now that the intent was that none of us would leave here alive today. I had to find a way to get all of us out of that house. That damn clock that I was warned about in times past had to be right at the witching hour. If I was right, we had almost no time left if we hoped to remain alive.

I am sure that Kathleen was able to read the look of fear that covered my face. She turned and looked at me. She was shaking, but I once again saw that "she-bear" characteristic in her. The children's lives were in danger and Kathleen would do anything to protect them. I quietly signaled to her and we moved towards the bedroom window. I slowly opened it and wanted Kathleen to leave first, but she refused.

"The children first," she whispered.

So, I lifted Melissa up and helped her out the window, once again kissing her cheek as I did. She was trembling and crying, but I managed to convince her to remain as quiet as possible. Jalen was next. The little guy appeared to be in shock. His face was pale. His body was limp. His eyes bore an empty look. I kissed his cheek, also.

"When you get out," I whispered in Kathleen's ear, "take the children and run. Don't stop. Don't even look back. Just go. Get away from here. Once they realize you're gone, they'll come after you."

"And you?"

"I'll follow. Try to lead them in another direction. Just go, Kathleen. As quickly as possible."

Kathleen stood at the window, as I prepared to help her climb out. For just a moment, she stared into my eyes. I could not read her thoughts. The woman had every reason to hate me. As far as she was concerned, I had put her life and the lives of the children at risk. In that moment of time, despite the fact that I alone knew I had not done any of the things to put all of this in position, I felt an overwhelming responsibility to make up for what I had not even done. I saw nothing but innocence in the lives of Kathleen, Melissa, and Jalen.

Suddenly, without any warning, the bedroom door burst open. Two men rushed into the room. I could also hear a commotion outside. Someone was approaching the children.

I turned my head just in time to see the gun pointed directly at Kathleen. There was no warning for her to stop. No interest in getting her to back away from the window. I saw everything as if it were moving in slow motion. The finger on the trigger began to squeeze, the gun was directly zeroed in on Kathleen. She would die first.

Just as suddenly, everything within me went into action. All in one motion, I shoved Kathleen down onto the carpeted floor and threw my body into the spot where she had been—in the very spot where a leaden missile was headed. I could hear Kathleen's scream. The sound of a gunshot followed the piercing pain in my body as the first bullet reached its target. I thought I heard additional shots, but I was already entering into that other zone, that place of no return. Something within me seemingly sensed that I could not survive what was happening now. A second bullet struck me and the pain was so intense, I wanted it to stop.

It did when the next bullet struck and everything went black.

I don't know how much time had transpired. I don't know where I had been. Now, I had no idea where I was. My eyes opened and slowly began to focus. I could sense that someone was standing close to the bed that I was lying in. At first, everything was a blur—kind of like looking through a pair of binoculars before making the adjustments to bring clarity to your sight.

Then I spotted a pair of eyeglasses hanging from a chain about the person's neck. Slowly, very slowly, the name tag came into sight. "Doris M. Sharpely, R.N."

I lifted my eyes further and caught sight once again of the elderly woman with the gray warm and friendly eyes I had seen previously, though at first, I could not recall where or when I had.

"Well, hello, Mr. Norman," the soft voice stated. "So, you've finally decided to come back to us, have you? Everything is going to be just fine, sir. Please remain still, while I summon the doctor."

The woman reached over for a cord and pressed a button several times. Then, she moved her face closer to mine and gently placed the palm of her hand on my face.

"Welcome back, Mr. Norman. Welcome back. We've been waiting for you."

Doctor Mildred Geldman was a pretty woman with dark black hair, green eyes, and a warm smile. She was at my bedside now and placed her stethoscope against my body. She had ready access to my pulse, heartbeat, body temperature, and blood pressure from the digital readouts on the monitor near my bed.

"Mr. Norman, I am Doctor Geldman. I want you to remain calm and please do not be alarmed. You have been in a comatose state for quite some time, sir. The fact that you have come out of that is very encouraging."

Doctor Geldman smiled.

"So nice to have you back again, sir."

My first attempts to speak failed. The doctor and nurse at my bedside could readily see the effort I was making.

"Just relax, Mr. Norman," Doctor Geldman said. "It may take some time for your body to catch up with things, but we have no reason to believe that all your functions will not return in due time."

Nurse Sharpely had a cup with a straw, water, and some ice chips in it. She picked it up, looked at the doctor, and received a nod to proceed. The liquid felt cool and refreshing against my parched lips and throat.

I tried to speak again and this time had some success.

"W-where?"

That was when I was told that I was in the Maple Grove Hospital in Minnesota.

"Bull ... bullet w-wounds," I uttered. "Sh-shot. Th-they sh-shot me. Kath-Kathleen ... the kids?"

I started to lift my head from the pillow, while Doctor Geldman gently pushed me back. She smiled.

"No bullet wounds, Mr. Norman. No one shot you. You've had a severe head injury. You likely had dreams and the mind can play such tricks on us."

Doctor Geldman did not even comment about Kathleen or the children, as I'm sure none of that meant anything to her or to Doris Sharpely.

"You're going to be fine, Mr. Norman. You will need to be patient and give your body some time to continue to heal and restore itself.

And you can be sure that we will be here to help you in every way possible."

I continued to lie there taking in my surroundings as Doctor Geldman examined me and gave some instructions to Nurse Sharpely. I heard mention of an MRI and some other tests, but, for the most part, my mind had already wandered back to Florida, Kathleen, Melissa, and Jalen. I remembered a man named Piscatulli and some thugs that killed two federal marshals and then came after Kathleen, the children, and me. Where was Avery Douglas now? Or did the man even exist? Had any of these things ever even occurred? Everything seemed so real, so vivid in my admittedly confused mind.

So that explained everything. There was no body switching. I never switched places with a man named Avery Douglas. This was all an incredible fantasy that my mind entered into while I hovered between worlds in a comatose state from which no one knew whether I would ever return. Sure. I heard about people who remained in a coma for years, until they finally died, never having regained consciousness. Where were they during all that time? The very thought of that frightened me.

When I was purportedly caught up in a fantasy that I was Avery Douglas and living with Kathleen and two children, I desperately wanted to escape from that world. When I found myself dealing with underworld figures and federal agents, I was frightened, intimidated, and unsure what I should do. When I imagined that I had a wife and two children who had all been placed in a dangerous position by the man whose body I inhabited, I felt the shame and frustration of being the man who had put their lives in jeopardy.

Now, as I lay in a hospital bed, realizing that I was exactly where I had been since the day paramedics first rushed me to the hospital following a serious car accident, I felt empty and purposeless. In a sense, in a crazy kind of way, I wanted to be back where I was when I was Avery Douglas ... uh ... minus the life threats against a wife and children and bullets riddling my body.

Everything seemed to come to a head and I started to cry. I didn't even fully understand why. I just turned my head to the side and sobbed.

Chapter Thirteen

Ugh! Rehabilitation

W eeks passed. I was no longer unconscious and the question of whether I would ever come out of a comatose state had been answered. But, muscles had atrophied and so many things that I had learned to do since childhood were in need of repair and restitution.

I was moved to a new location, the St. Mark's Rehabilitation Center in New Hope, just about five miles from Maple Grove. New Hope—the name of the city was promising, but I can't say that I bore a great deal of hope at the time. I was immediately put through a rigorous series of exercises and therapy. I was learning again how to walk, how to use my hands in meaningful ways, how to speak clearly, how to read and exercise my mind. Some of this was painful. Some things were coming very slowly, if at all. Some were humiliating for a grown man.

Sometimes, I questioned whether any of this was even worth the effort. I knew that I was reaching a point where I honestly didn't care if I improved or not. My life was empty. I was a prisoner once again, no longer in a fictitious other man's body, but now in a rehab center where I was still closed off from the real world and incapable of being the man I once was.

I didn't watch television. I was still unable to read without the words swimming around and sliding off a page. I felt so helpless, so useless. I'd spent a few months living in some crazy fantasy and now, when I was back to reality, my life was not one-bit better. During the day, I'd struggle just to do normal, everyday activities. At night, I dreamt of a woman named Kathleen and two children who once thought I was their daddy. In my fantasy life, I was running from mobsters and federal agents. In my reality life, I didn't run at all. I had enough difficulty just trying to walk.

The rehabilitation center I was in was a pleasant enough place, other than the fact that it was kind of like a hospital with a bit more activity. I did like to sit outside in what was a garden, courtyard area with a fountain that fed into a small pond with some large attractive fish swimming freely. I actually admired their effortless movement.

And that's where I was when Penny Henderson, one of the staff members came looking for me. I didn't need to always be in a wheel chair, but I was in one on this day. My physical therapy that day had been pretty grueling, making my legs tired and achy. Gordon James, another staff member, suggested I use the chair so that I could move around in the courtyard without overly straining myself.

"We have a guest asking to see you, Jeff. Molly is bringing your guest in now. Just wanted to give you a heads up."

Then, someone called out to Penny and she quickly moved away to assist them.

A guest? To date, the only guests to ever come and see me were Doris Sharpely, who stopped in one day on her way home from work; George Felton, my shift supervisor from UPS; my employer; and two of the UPS drivers, Linda Pritchard and Frank Solomon.

I appreciated anyone's kind gesture in checking in on me, but, to be perfectly honest, I was still self-conscious about my physical limitations. I couldn't stand up very easily on my own, my mind was still somewhat hazy and slow at times, and sometimes it took me longer than normal to get the words out that I wanted to say.

I could see Molly approaching from a distance, but I could not make out who the person was walking with her. When they got close enough and I was able to see them more clearly, it's a wonder I didn't pass out and fall out of the wheelchair.

"Hey, Jeff, I believe you two know each other, so I'm gonna leave you guys alone and let you spend some time together."

This time I was beyond simply struggling to get the words out that I wanted to say. I couldn't seem to get a single syllable out.

"I told them that you and I are close friends who've known each other for years and that I just learned that you were out of the coma and here at this center. I know that was very presumptuous of me and you would have no idea who I am, but I ... I just had to come and follow up on ... on something very important to me. Please forgive me. I hope you are feeling better, sir, and that your recovery will be speedy and all."

I was breathing so heavily and striving so hard to even make a sound. I cannot think of any other time in my life when I so wanted to say something and was unable to do so.

"Listen. I am so sorry for coming here and disturbing you like this. Please forgive me. I hope that I have not upset you. I know I must sound like some kind of crazy person to you, but I'm really not. I just needed to know. I was quite sure that the whole idea was crazy, but ..."

She started to rise when I finally made a sound.

"Kath-Kathleen."

Her head spun back as she stared at me. Her eyes were as wide as saucers. Her mouth was open. Her knees went slack, forcing her to sit back down for a moment.

"Kathleen," I said again and, as I did, her eyes filled with tears.

"Y-you know me? Did they tell you? Did they tell you my name before I got out here?"

I felt a clarity move in throughout my mind. It was like a fresh springtime breeze passing through me. I smiled, reached over, and placed a hand on top of hers.

"No one ... no one would have to tell me your name, Kathleen. Wh-why should they have to? Of course, I know you ... How could I not?"

Kathleen just sat there staring at me. She was shaking her head and breathing much faster than she had been. Now, she was the one struggling for words.

"I'm s-so glad that you came, Kathleen. Th-the children, Melissa and Jalen. Tell me ...are th-they okay? How are they?"

The two of us sat quietly together under the shade of an elm tree. We were holding hands and much more relaxed with each other. Kathleen did most of the talking and that's when I learned all that had happened.

Avery Douglas was dead. He died near the bedroom window of a safe house, shot to death by two of Antonio Piscatulli's guys. But, even as the bullets struck Douglas, the two shooters were cut down by FBI Agent Stephen Sundberry, who had arrived at the scene along with several other FBI agents. They had become aware that three of Piscatulli's thugs were posing as Bureau agents and planned to kill Avery Douglas and his family. First, Piscatulli's men killed the two federal marshals who had come for Kathleen and the children.

I also learned that the FBI had clear evidence that Piscatulli was behind the murders of the federal marshals and he had already been arrested and charged with first degree murder of two federal agents—crimes that carried a death penalty, if convicted. The feds still had the evidence of money laundering that I provided on a flash drive and Kathleen said that someone else at Avery's office had been arrested. I assumed that was none other than Arthur Vaughn.

I started to ask all sorts of questions when Kathleen placed a finger on my lips and stopped me from speaking. She edged a bit closer to me, smiled, and stared into my eyes.

"Jeff, I need to know. I'll answer every question you have, I promise. But first, I have something I have to ask you."

I was a bit surprised at the seriousness of the tone of her voice, but I knew that whatever was on her mind was of the utmost importance to her. I recalled how incredibly kind and gracious Kathleen was and the fact that she had been so victimized by her husband. I wanted, more than anything, to help her with whatever was troubling her.

It's a strange thing, but, just moments before, I was struggling to even speak to this woman and my mind was still fuzzy and unclear. Now, as I sat there and stared back into her eyes, I felt so refreshed, so renewed, and strong.

"If you are who you say you are, then you know that we were together on the last night before Avery was shot. You were trying to convince me that you were really Jeff Norman.

You said something very special to me during that time. Can you repeat those words that you said to me? Can you tell me what you said to me on that very last night when we were together?"

In that moment of time, Kathleen appeared to be so innocent, so vulnerable, as she sat there before me. And amazingly, I knew ... I knew, in an instant, what Kathleen was referring to. My response flowed freely with no hesitation at all. I stared deeply into her eyes.

"I told you that in another time and another place, I would love you ... I would love you with every fiber of my being."

Those same crystal-clear globules that I had seen once before, filled her eyes and began to gently glide down her face. She took both my hands in hers and moved her lips so close to mine that I could feel her breath entering my mouth.

Despite the tears, a smile covered her face.

"Jeff Norman, *this is another time and another place.*"

And then her lips were upon mine and I felt it. It was a power, a force, some kind of magic that I had never before known or experienced. It had to be what happens when two soul mates have found each other and share their very first kiss. It had to be that moment when a dream comes true, when something birthed deeply within your soul comes to fruition.

We kissed again and soon our tears were also kissing each other as I was now crying. This time, however, we were sharing tears of joy.

Chapter Fourteen

And So It Goes

Six months have passed since the day Kathleen came back into my life. I am no longer a patient in a rehabilitation center. In fact, I am no longer in Minnesota.

Kathleen and I were married in a quiet ceremony three weeks ago and we are still getting settled in our new home in Milton, Florida, a city just outside Pensacola. Melissa and Jalen are already enrolled in school and Kathleen and I are still taking our time unloading boxes.

The home we acquired is a three bedroom, two bath ranch located on a cul-de-sac in a quiet neighborhood. It's not even in the same league as the home Kathleen had with Avery over on Florida's east coast—she lost that one as a part of the settlement to pay off Avery's ill-gotten funds and money owed to the IRS—but Kathleen doesn't seem the least bit bothered by any of that. I can hear her humming softly each time she puts her personal touch on decorating a room or placing certain items where she would like them to be.

Between some savings I had accumulated over the years, money I had in my UPS profit sharing, and money I derived from the sale of my condo, I was certainly not left destitute after my accident. My insurance carriers covered my medical expenses, my car was replaced, and I am on permanent disability and receive a monthly stipend. I walk with a cane and, sometimes, for shorter jaunts, I forego that walking stick. I have never fully regained full dexterity in my left hand, but I do okay. I mean, hey, I can cut my own steak and help Kathleen with the dishes without dropping a single plate or cup. And I can play catch with Jalen.

Kathleen was left with pretty much nothing after Avery Douglas' criminal activities were accounted for and that process is still in the hands of lawyers and accountants. But. Kathleen did derive half million dollars from a life insurance policy that Avery had. I convinced her to immediately set up a trust to cover the kids' future educational expenses, which she did. She invested a smaller portion of the payoff and then took remaining funds and joined them with mine. We entered into our marriage with a commitment that we would start our lives anew, share everything, and build towards the future. We have also started the process of me adopting Melissa and Jalen. And, yes, we have already enrolled Melissa in dance classes here in our new community, and Jalen is signed up for baseball and soccer.

I will never understand what happened the day that I somehow switched identities with a man named Avery Douglas. I am also convinced that there is no one in this world, or, at least, no one I can even think of, who can explain how that ever occurred. And I must admit, there are times when the very thought of that ever happening to me again scares me beyond measure.

But it did happen. I know it did. And now, Kathleen, the one person that I most needed to also know, does.

"You saved my life that day," Kathleen has said, "and I saw how hard you were fighting to save Melissa and Jalen. You could have abandoned us, run away somewhere, claimed that we were not your responsibility, but you never did."

Kathleen told me that after Avery was dead and her world was being torn apart as the crimes of her husband were being revealed, she could not shake the conversation we had on that last night. She also said so many other things started to flash through her mind.

"I remembered the day you agreed to go to dinner together and let the children choose the restaurant. That was so incredibly 'un-Avery-like'," she said. "The way you talked with the children that night and turned your cell phone off. The manner in which you ordered your steak and the fact that you suddenly hated mushrooms."

Kathleen laughed at her own words.

"At first, I assumed you were changing because of a head injury or a near-death experience, but some of the things I was noticing were not merely changes in personality or mannerisms. They seemed to be things coming from a completely different person. You were nothing like you used to be. Even the way you began to look at me was beyond anything I had ever received from Avery, even when we first met. I think I knew even back then that he wanted me for his 'trophy wife,' while he had other women on the side."

I've decided to not even try to comprehend how or why any of this ever happened. I could cite reasons such as I was sent into Avery's body to save the lives of Kathleen and the children, but that only raises additional unanswerable questions. Sent by whom? Why me? Why did it happen in this instance, when it has not happened to other people?

Or has it? Are there others walking on this planet who have experienced this same thing and, like me, tucked it away one day and simply moved on with their lives?

Okay, okay, enough of that. Let's reflect for a moment upon what I do know and know with certainty. I absolutely adore Kathleen, Melissa, and Jalen and have been rewarded with a life beyond my wildest imagination and deepest dreams.

It happened. It all happened just as I have recounted. And I am so incredibly thankful that it did.

I am a man who once had two identities, two lives. I have only one life now—and I love everything about it.

The End

FROM THE AUTHOR:

T hank you for reading *ID: The Man with Two Lives.* I had a great deal of enjoyment writing this novella. When I worked within my profession as an attorney, most everything I wrote was rather stiff and constrained. As a novelist, I have been able to break away from all that fettered me and write on a much greater level of freedom and imagination. My goal is to provide you, the reader, with as much enjoyment as I enjoy when creating a work.

If you enjoyed this, please consider providing a review online. Even a short statement that you really liked this helps immensely. Thanks.

Please visit my author website at:
www.vincentsachar.com.

Also, we love hearing from our readers and invite you to receive occasional updates from us. Feel free to contact as at vsach777@gmail.com

ABOUT THE AUTHOR:

V incent J. Sachar is an attorney with a passion for writing fiction. He earned his Juris Doctor from St. John's Law School in New York. Vince is also an experienced public speaker. In addition to speaking at book events, book clubs, author meet & greet events, author panels, and more, he has addressed crowds large and small (sometimes with foreign language interpreters) and has done so in very unique situations (including at a prison in Siberia).

Sachar also conducts radio and internet interviews across the nation and has provided interviews for prominent author websites.

Vince and his wife, Gwen, also speak at high schools, colleges and universities.

To learn more, please visit Vince's author site: www.vincentsachar.com

www.ingramcontent.com/pod-product-compliance
Lightning Source LLC
Chambersburg PA
CBHW070223140626
46555CB00018B/1258